"I dare you to read a 'Kurland' story and not enjoy it."
—Heartland Critiques

Praise for

To Kiss in the Shadows . . .

"A heroine graced with gentle humor and an indomitable spirit . . . A fine example of Ms. Kurland's writing style."
—Heartstrings Reviews

"Delightful [and] very unusual . . . Sweet, loving, amusing, exciting, and passionate." *—A Romance Review*

"An action-packed adventure."
—The Romance Readers Connection

"[Kurland] writes with warmth and wit." *—Romantic Times*

"A treat." *—The Best Reviews*

. . . and the novels of USA Today *bestselling author Lynn Kurland*

Dreams of Stardust

"Kurland weaves another fabulous read with just the right amounts of laughter, romance, and fantasy."
—Affaire de Coeur

A Garden in the Rain

"Kurland laces her exquisitely romantic, utterly bewitching blend of contemporary romance and time travel with a delectable touch of tart wit, leaving readers savoring every word of this superbly written romance." *—Booklist*

"Kurland is clearly one of romance's finest writers—she consistently delivers the kind of stories readers dream about. Don't miss this one." *—The Oakland Press*

continued . . .

From This Moment On

"A disarming blend of romance, suspense, and heartwarming humor, this book is romantic comedy at its best."

—*Publishers Weekly*

"A deftly plotted delight, seasoned with a wonderfully wry sense of humor and graced with endearing, unforgettable characters, including a trio of healer-witches, a rough-around-the-edges hero who can't understand why all his fiancées flee or faint at the sight of him, and a heroine who discovers she is stronger than she ever imagined."

—*Booklist*

My Heart Stood Still

"Written with poetic grace and a wickedly subtle sense of humor . . . the essence of pure romance. Sweet, poignant, and truly magical, this is a rare treat: a romance with characters readers will come to care about and a love story they will cherish."

—*Booklist*

"A totally enchanting tale, sensual and breathtaking . . . An absolute must-read."

—*Rendezvous*

If I Had You

"Kurland brings history to life . . . in this tender medieval romance."

—*Booklist*

"A passionate story filled with danger, intrigue, and sparkling dialogue."

—*Rendezvous*

The More I See You

"The superlative Ms. Kurland once again wows her readers with her formidable talent as she weaves a tale of enchantment that blends history with spellbinding passion and impressive characterization, not to mention a magnificent plot."

—*Rendezvous*

Another Chance to Dream

"Kurland creates a special romance between a memorable knight and his lady." —*Publishers Weekly*

The Very Thought of You

"[A] masterpiece . . . this fabulous tale will enchant anyone who reads it." —*Painted Rock Reviews*

This Is All I Ask

"An exceptional read." —*The Atlanta Journal-Constitution*

"Both powerful and sensitive . . . a wonderfully rich and rewarding book." —Susan Wiggs

"A medieval of stunning intensity. Sprinkled with adventure, fantasy, and heart, *This Is All I Ask* reaches outside the boundaries of romance to embrace every thoughtful reader, every person of feeling." —Christina Dodd

A Dance Through Time

"An irresistibly fast and funny romp across time." —Stella Cameron

"Lynn Kurland's vastly entertaining time travel treats us to a delightful hero and heroine . . . a humorous novel of feisty fun and adventure." —*A Little Romance*

"Her heroes are delightful . . . A wonderful read!" —*Heartland Critiques*

Titles by Lynn Kurland

STARDUST OF YESTERDAY
A DANCE THROUGH TIME
THIS IS ALL I ASK
THE VERY THOUGHT OF YOU
ANOTHER CHANCE TO DREAM
THE MORE I SEE YOU
IF I HAD YOU
MY HEART STOOD STILL
FROM THIS MOMENT ON
A GARDEN IN THE RAIN
DREAMS OF STARDUST
MUCH ADO ABOUT MOONLIGHT

Anthologies

CHRISTMAS SPIRITS
(with Casey Claybourne, Elizabeth Bevarly, and Jenny Lykins)

THE CHRISTMAS CAT
(with Julie Beard, Barbara Bretton, and Jo Beverley)

VEILS OF TIME
(with Maggie Shayne, Angie Ray, and Ingrid Weaver)

OPPOSITES ATTRACT
(with Elizabeth Bevarly, Emily Carmichael, and Elda Minger)

LOVE CAME JUST IN TIME

A KNIGHT'S VOW
(with Patricia Potter, Deborah Simmons, and Glynnis Campbell)

TAPESTRY
(with Madeline Hunter, Sherrilyn Kenyon, and Karen Marie Moning)

THE QUEEN IN WINTER
(with Sharon Shinn, Claire Delacroix, Sarah Monette)

To Kiss in the Shadows

Lynn Kurland

THE BERKLEY PUBLISHING GROUP
Published by the Penguin Group
Penguin Group (USA) Inc.
375 Hudson Street, New York, New York 10014, USA
Penguin Group (Canada), 90 Eglinton Avenue East, Suite 700, Toronto, Ontario M4P 2Y3, Canada
(a division of Pearson Penguin Canada Inc.)
Penguin Books Ltd., 80 Strand, London WC2R 0RL, England
Penguin Group Ireland, 25 St. Stephen's Green, Dublin 2, Ireland (a division of Penguin Books Ltd.)
Penguin Group (Australia), 250 Camberwell Road, Camberwell, Victoria 3124, Australia
(a division of Pearson Australia Group Pty. Ltd.)
Penguin Books India Pvt. Ltd., 11 Community Centre, Panchsheel Park, New Delhi—110 017, India
Penguin Group (NZ), Cnr. Airborne and Rosedale Roads, Albany, Auckland 1310, New Zealand
(a division of Pearson New Zealand Ltd.)
Penguin Books (South Africa) (Pty.) Ltd., 24 Sturdee Avenue, Rosebank, Johannesburg 2196,
South Africa

Penguin Books Ltd., Registered Offices: 80 Strand, London WC2R 0RL, England

Previously included in the anthology *Tapestry*, published by Jove Books, an imprint of The Berkley Publishing Group.

TO KISS IN THE SHADOWS

A Berkley Book / published by arrangement with the author

PRINTING HISTORY
Berkley edition / September 2006

ISBN: 0-425-21063-4

BERKLEY®
Berkley Books are published by The Berkley Publishing Group,
a division of Penguin Group (USA) Inc.,
375 Hudson Street, New York, New York 10014.
BERKLEY is a registered trademark of Penguin Group (USA) Inc.
The "B" design is a trademark belonging to Penguin Group (USA) Inc.

PRINTED IN THE UNITED STATES OF AMERICA

10 9 8 7 6 5 4 3 2 1

One

'Tis said that in a woman's solar the course of wars and the fate of countries is decided.

'Tis also said that therein is determined the fate of men and the manner of their course to a woman's bed.

Lianna of Grasleigh suspected that a woman had said the former and a man the latter, for 'twas a certainty that no man she knew would have accorded a woman the cleverness to determine the destiny of his realm. But if any man had heard the plotting and scheming going on behind her, he would have perhaps thought differently. At the very least, he would have quivered in fear for the fate of his own poor soul.

"Bind him," suggested the first of the other women in the solar.

"Nay, lure him," said the second.

"Help him slip into his cups, lure him, and *then* bind him," said the third. Then she gulped in surprise, as if that thought were too bold a one to voice.

Lianna let the peat smoke, perfumed oils, and stratagem flow over her. She had no stomach for joining in the talk—not that the ladies behind her would have allowed it. A member of court though she might be by command of the king, she was not accepted by that court. It had troubled her at first, that shunning, but she had grown accustomed to it. Besides, 'twas better that she keep to the work under her hands. Let the tapestry of the court be woven without her single thread running through it. She had her own pattern to see to.

She tilted her frame to catch the final shaft of sunlight that bravely entered the chamber despite the daunting thickness of the walls. To have fully succeeded in seeing her work, she would have had to turn her face to the women behind her, but that she could not do. Instead, she sat with her back to the chamber and made do with less light than was needful.

Much as she did in her life.

"Lie in wait for him," said the first. "In the passageway, where he must speak as he passes."

"Lie in wait in his bed," corrected the second with a lusty laugh, "and then see if he can pass on such an invitation."

"I would lie anywhere," said the third breathlessly. "Mayhap he would tread upon me."

"He will not be trapped by such simple ploys," said a fourth voice in a tone that cut through the speculation like a sword through living flesh.

Silence descended, silence broken only by Lianna's needle as it pierced the cloth again and again. She was powerfully tempted to look over her shoulder and see the looks the other women—save the one who had spoken in the end, of course—were wearing fixed to their no-doubt quite pale visages. But drawing their attention would only draw the attention of their sharp tongues as well, so she forbore. Perhaps listening to what she was certain would be a severe rebuke would be amusement enough for the afternoon.

"Kendrick of Artane will not be trapped by foolish gels who have no head for strategies," Maud of Harrow said, and she said it so decidedly that only a fool would have dared argue with her. "He is cunning and shrewd. To catch him, one must be his equal in stealth."

"But," said the woman who had spoken first, sounding rather hesitant, "would he not find it unpleasing to have a woman as full of wit as he?"

Lianna stitched contentedly. Adela was certainly lacking in wit, so that would not be a problem for her.

"I still say it matters not what wits you have, if you have enough of them to find yourself betwixt his sheets," said Janet, Adela's sister, whose most heartfelt desire seemed to be to find herself betwixt sheets—anyone's sheets—as often as possible.

"I agree," said the third timidly. She was Linet of Byford, and of the women behind her, the least vicious, to Lianna's mind. At least Linet flinched when Maud's tongue began to cut. "Surely," Linet continued, "his preference is a woman warm and willing in his bed."

"Many women have tried," said Maud, "but he refuses them all. Nay, the way to have him must come from a more subtle attack."

And how would Maud know? Lianna wondered. Perhaps she had given the matter much thought in an effort to find a diversion from her own terrible straits. And why not, given the life she had? The woman was wed to a man with a tongue so cruel few could bear him. Lianna shuddered. Had she been wed to such a man, she soon would have been reduced to cowering in the corner, of that she was certain.

Maud never cowered, not even before her lord. Then again, her tongue was as sharp as his. Lianna knew this because she'd listened to Maud use that weapon on her vile husband more than once. And, of course, she'd felt the bite of it herself—which was part of the reason she placed herself with her back to the chamber. There was little to be gained by giving Maud or her companions a constant view of her ruined visage. Maud tormented her enough while facing naught but her back.

But none of that explained how Maud knew so much about Kendrick of Artane's habits. Had she tried to have him in the past and failed? Did she intend to try again now? She was at Henry's court whilst her husband was off on an errand for the king in France. Mayhap she considered this a perfect time to trot out a new strategy.

"We might have more success with his brother," Linet offered timidly. "The one still free. The youngest."

The numerous swift intakes of breath were startling. Then there was absolute silence for the space of several heartbeats.

"Jason of Artane?" Maud asked. Her voice could have been full of what another might have termed fear.

Lianna was so surprised, she ventured a look over her shoulder. To her astonishment, Maud looked as frightened as the rest of the women.

"He isn't of Artane," Linet said. "Well, he was. But now he is of Blackmour."

And the women, as one, crossed themselves.

Lianna wondered if she might have passed too much time during her youth with her face pressed against linen to judge its usefulness for her stitching purposes. Obviously, she had missed several delicious rumors.

"The Dragon of Blackmour's squire," Adela agreed.

"You're a fool, sister. Jason de Piaget is the Dragon's *former* squire," Janet corrected. "He's his own man now. And likely as full of evil habits as the old worm himself."

"I hear he's handsome," Linet ventured.

"He was trained by Blackmour, who we know is a warlock," Maud said crisply. "No doubt Lord Jason, as fair of face as he might be, mastered many dark arts at his master's hand. Would you sell your frivolous souls to such a man in return for his deadly kisses?"

There was a bit of low murmuring, as if the other women considered it. Lianna was spared further speculation by the abrupt bursting open of the door.

"He's here!" a body announced breathlessly.

"Jason?" Linet asked with a gasp, sounding so terrified that Lianna could only assume she had reflected a bit more on Maud's words.

"Nay, Kendrick," the voice from the door said. "He's here!"

"Have you seen him?" Maud demanded.

"Nay, but I heard tell—"

Apparently, that was enough for the women, even Maud, though Lianna wondered what Maud's husband would say when he returned from his journeys and found out his wife was pursuing one of the most sought-after knights in the realm. For herself, Lianna was unsurprised by Maud's actions. She had ceased to be appalled by wedded women hunting desirable, unwedded men, even though in her home such a thing would have been unthinkable. Her parents had been devoted to each other. The thought of her mother having looked at a man other than her father never would have occurred to Lianna.

Of course, that was before, before her family had been slain, before she had been fetched by the king's courtiers and brought to court, where she had seen many things she never would have believed possible. 'Twas little wonder she passed most of her waking hours in the queen's least-used solar, hiding from the intrigues and horrors of court, and trying desperately with needle and thread to recapture some of the beauty she'd lost.

The door banged shut, and the excited shrieks of the women faded. Silence descended swiftly, leaving Lianna with nothing to face but her own thoughts. She looked over at the window and marked with dismay the waning of the daylight. Dusk meant she would have to descend to the great hall and take her place at the king's table.

How she loathed evenings! A pity she couldn't hide herself in some darkened corner of the hall. Nay, her place was determined by the vastness of her father's holdings.

She often wondered why Henry hadn't kept those lands for his own, but perhaps he had enough to fret over without them. Far better to sell her and her soil to a man who could manage the both of them. The king had need enough of allies, and she, after six months at court, had few illusions about what her fate would be. Her only surprise was that she hadn't met that fate yet. Surely her freedom couldn't last much longer. Even she was old enough, and wise enough, at a score to understand that.

But even though her holdings and her station guaranteed her a place at supper, they didn't guarantee her freedom from stares and smirks.

Would that they could.

The door behind her opened softly. She sighed but didn't turn her head. That was something else she'd learned at Henry's court: to hide her face. Tongues were cruel and never more so than when gazing on her poor visage. Better a knife in her back than words to pierce her soul.

There was a substantial pause, then a soft footfall that came her way. Lianna ducked her head. A long form settled across from her on one of the stone benches set into the wall. Lianna glanced up long enough to see that it was a man, but not one dressed in the trappings of a lord. Given his clothing, he was nothing more than a squire, and a poor one at that. She had nothing to fear from such a man. She could dismiss him easily.

She bent her head to her stitchery. "You shouldn't be here," she said firmly.

"Aye, there's a goodly bit of truth," he said with feeling. "The saints preserve me from the intrigues of a woman's solar."

Given that such had been her thoughts as well, she risked a look at the man facing her. And the beauty of his visage, even cast as it was in the last rays of sunlight, was enough to make her catch her breath.

His breath caught as well, and a small sound of dismay escaped him. But that brief flash of pity was gone so quickly, she almost wondered if she'd imagined it. He smiled a smile that would have felled her instantly had she not been so firmly seated on her chair.

"The pox," he noted. "I had it, too. I'll show you my scars, if you like."

She blinked at him.

"They aren't on my sweet visage, as you can see."

She made a strangled noise of denial, hoping fervently that the man wouldn't feel the need to strip down to his altogether to ensure her comfort.

His smile turned into a mischievous grin that had her smiling in return—regardless of any desire she might have had to do otherwise.

"Your maidenly eyes are safe," he promised with a wink. He stretched out his long legs. "Who are you?" he asked. "And where are your fellows?"

"Lianna of Grasleigh," she answered promptly, then realized that perhaps giving an unknown man her name wasn't wise. "And the ladies are coming back immediately," she added hastily.

"Off hunting, are they?" he asked.

"Hunting?"

"Aye," he said easily. "I know their kind. Always after some poor fool or other."

"The poor fool for the afternoon is Kendrick of Artane," she said with a scowl. "The handsome, wealthy, apparently infinitely desirable Kendrick of Artane."

"You seem to know much of him."

"I've been forced to listen to a listing of his virtues for the past se'nnight."

"But surely you must believe the reports," he said.

"How could one man be so perfect?" she asked. "I daresay the tales are magnified far beyond the truth." She listened to herself and was surprised to find that her courage was magnified far beyond its usual bounds. Speaking so freely to anyone not of her family wasn't her habit. Perhaps her tongue had reached its limit in patience.

"And what are those tales?" he asked, looking quite interested. "I've always a ready ear for ladies' gossip."

Lianna jabbed her needle into the cloth with vigor. Why not? If he had nothing better to do than listen, she had little better to do than talk. Besides, he wasn't laughing at her, nor was he insulting her. For that alone he deserved to be indulged. Perhaps he, too, sought only a respite before the torture of supper.

She let her needle fall and watched as the thread untwisted. "They say," she said, picking the needle back up, "that he has a visage to rival any angel's and a smile to set an abbess swooning into his arms."

"Sounds unlikely."

"Aye," she agreed. "Of course, that is but the beginning. They say he has seduced so many women to his bed that he's lost count and skewered so many of their lords on his sword that the blade won't surrender the bloodstains."

"Poetic," he said with a sigh. "Truly."

"That he has bedded so many?" she asked sharply. "Or that he has slain so many?"

"The latter, surely, but the first is more interesting."

"How so?"

He shrugged. "A man does what he must in matters of love."

"Better that he had denied himself now and again."

The man lifted one eyebrow. "The pleasures of a woman's bed? Think you?"

"If he has no control over his passions before he weds, how will he have any after he weds? Should he manage to distract some daft wench long enough to drag her before a priest, that is."

The man laughed. "You've given his bride much thought, I see."

"Aye, poor girl." She pursed her lips. "Surely she would expect more from him than so many indiscretions."

The man looked at her thoughtfully for a moment or two, then shrugged. "For all you know, tales of his prowess are false."

"Are they?" she asked skeptically.

"Tell me the tales, then let me judge. There are more reports of his antics, aren't there?" he asked hopefully.

"Aye. Enough to nauseate you for days."

"Tell on, then. I can hardly wait to hear them."

Who was she to deny this poor fool his little pleasures? She picked out the last handful of stitches she'd put in awry, then carried on with the gossip she'd heard over the past handful of days.

" 'Tis said," she continued, "that he consorts with all manner of odd folk, from faeries to warlocks. He has unholy skill with his blade. He escapes from impossible perils and emerges from all battles unscathed."

The man laughed. "By the saints, what a fanciful bit of fluff. Now, if bogles and ghosties are your fancy, rather you should concentrate on his younger brother. 'Tis Jason who consorts with warlocks and other such horrors. I daresay Kendrick, poor lad, hasn't the stomach for such things. Rather, he no doubt finds himself more comfortable in the pleasant and undemanding company of women."

"Then he'd best not come here," Lianna muttered, "for this collection of shrews is anything but undemanding."

"Perhaps with luck he'll avoid them," he said. "And you, lady, are you able to avoid them?"

Lianna wove her needle into the cloth to hold it, then rubbed her eyes with a sigh. "If only I could—"

A sudden commotion at the door made the man spring to his feet and pull the hood of his cloak close around his face. Lianna looked over her shoulder to find Maud and her companions sweeping back into the chamber as if they'd been royalty. And royalty, Lianna knew, was what they most certainly were not. Indeed, they were lower in station than her mother had been—making them lower in station than she herself was.

Yet another reason for them to hate her.

Maud looked at Lianna's companion. "This is a woman's solar, you fool. Who gave you permission to enter?"

" 'Twas a mistake, my lady," the man said, bobbing his head respectfully.

"Or did you invite him?"

Lianna realized Maud was glaring at her only because she felt the heat of the other woman's gaze. Perhaps the gossips had it wrong. Jason of Artane might have consorted with witches and warlocks, but he was likely just a man and possessed no unearthly powers. Maud, however, seemed to be fair burning a hole in Lianna's head with her gaze alone, which led Lianna to wonder about whom the woman really consorted with in the dead of night.

And by the time she'd thought that through, she found Maud's clawlike grasp encircling her wrist. Maud hauled her to her feet.

"How one as ugly as you could entice a man, I don't know," Maud said harshly, "but you'll not sully my solar with your whorish ways. This will teach you your place."

Lianna watched as Maud's other hand came toward her face. She'd never been struck in her life, and she could scarce believe it was going to happen to her now. The other thought that occurred to her was that this wasn't Maud's solar. It was the queen's solar, but since the queen was not at the keep, the right of the place likely should have gone to the woman of highest rank.

Which, as it happened, was Lianna herself.

Maud's hand continued toward her face. Lianna winced in anticipation of the blow.

A blow which never came.

Lianna opened her eyes, realizing just then that she'd closed them, only to find Maud's hand caught in another larger and stronger grip.

"Do not," commanded the man.

"And who are you to stop me?" Maud spat.

The man flipped his hood back with his other hand and smiled pleasantly.

"Kendrick of Artane!" squeaked Linet. "By the saints, Maud, 'tis him!"

"Silence, you silly twit!" Maud hissed. "I *know* that."

Lianna's first act was to gape at him in astonishment. Then she latched onto the urge to slink back into a corner and hope that Kendrick would forget her and everything she'd said about him in the past quarter-hour. She pulled her other hand from Maud's slackened grip and backed away, feeling her cheeks grow suddenly quite hot. By the saints, she had thoroughly insulted the man—and to his face, no less!

She was spared the humiliation of having to look at him, however, because he stepped in front of her and spoke to the other women.

"Perhaps I might escort you ladies to supper. I understand His Majesty plans to lay an uncommonly fine table tonight, and no doubt you'll want to seek your places early."

"But," Maud protested, trying to step around him and finish what she'd started.

Indeed, Lianna saw her hand still twitching, as if it itched to slap her.

"There is nothing here that warrants your further attention, Lady Harrow. Aye, I recognized you from your sapphire-like eyes, didn't you know? Tales of your beauty precede you wherever you go."

Maud snorted in frustration, but Kendrick seemed not to notice.

"Let us be off," he said. "I can see nothing here that either you or I need mark any further, can you?"

Lianna wondered if she should be stung by his words or expect them. But as he with one hand dragged the women from the chamber, he was with the other giving her a friendly wave behind his back.

She watched them leave. The solar door shut firmly behind them. The relief that flooded through her was enough to weaken her knees. She sank into her chair, grateful and not a little bemused. She had just thoroughly insulted the most eligible knight of the realm, yet he had accorded her the gesture of a conspirator. And he had also rid her of her banes—at least for the moment. A pity she could not find such a man to wed her, that she might be forever without such scourges.

The thought of Kendrick of Artane wedding with such a one as she sent renewed color to her cheeks. He was too brilliant a star in the firmament. Even had she possessed her beauty still, she could not have borne him as a husband. She wanted to be far removed from court, from pitiless tongues wagging at her, from being forced to attend a king who had no use for her except that she was connected to her land.

Ah, that a man might come and rescue her, free her from the king's wardship, and take her home. A pity she could not find one who was even uglier than she, that he might be grateful to have her.

She looked at her stitchery, then ran her fingers over her work, over the dark threads that depicted the scene laced with shadows. At least in those shadows made of thread there was somewhere to hide. Perhaps that was all she dared hope for herself, a piece of shadow somewhere where she could hide and forget her ruined visage.

But if she hid in the shadows, how would any man find her?

She pushed her work aside, surprised at the foolishness of her thoughts. It mattered not whether she hid or stood in full sunlight; no man would ever want her. The poor fool who would eventually be forced to wed her would likely think his nuptials the blackest day of his life.

She rose, turned toward the door, and put her shoulders back. Dinner called and 'twould go worse for her if she were late, for then she would be noticed the more.

She left the solar with her head down.

Two

Jason of Artane rode through the barbican, cursing his father, his next older brother, and the weather, the last of which had been foul for the past pair of fortnights and was fair now only after he'd suffered out in it for a month. The early morning sunlight streamed down fiercely, as if it sought to pound good cheer into him with its rays. He stifled a hearty sneeze in his sleeve and wondered why he'd ever agreed to humor his father by following his brother from one end of the island to the other.

It had been a miserable journey from Artane, he had been sent on a useless errand to distract him from his true purpose, and he was certain he'd caught a healthy case of the ague the night before from having to sleep in a drafty stable instead of the nice warm inn he'd selected. He supposed he had only himself to blame for the latter. If he'd kept his cloak pulled together and his lips clamped shut, he wouldn't have been recognized. Instead, he'd given his name when asked and let his cloak fall away from the blood-red ruby in the hilt of his sword. The usual reaction had occurred.

Men had crossed themselves.

Women had screamed and fainted.

Jason had sighed in disgust, downed the tankard of ale he'd managed to obtain, flipped a coin to a speechless patron in return for the rough bread and hunk of cheese he had filched from him on his way out the door, then sought out the most comfortable part of a hayloft for his bed. Such, he'd supposed, was the lot of a man who had squired for the lord of Blackmour.

That lord would have found the tale vastly amusing.

Jason found the kink in his neck and his rapidly stuffing nose anything but.

He sneezed again as he rode into the bailey unchallenged. Guardsmen who would have demanded any other man's name merely gaped at him and weakly waved him past. Jason knew he should have been amused. After all, 'twas seldom that a man of a score and five had such a fiercesome reputation without having done much to deserve it.

It wasn't that he was a poor swordsman. Even he, modest though he considered himself to be, was well aware of his ability. One could not be the son of Robin of Artane and not have had some small talent for swordplay granted him. But whatever mastery he had of his blade, he had paid for himself by time spent in the lists.

He also didn't mind that the souls about him suspected him of all manner of dark habits. He had been first page, then squire, then willing guest of Christopher of Blackmour for most of his life. Some of the mystery surrounding the man had been bound to cloak Jason as well. He knew the true way of things, so idle gossip and charms spat out in haste when he passed didn't trouble him.

What did trouble him, though, was the fact that he'd finally found a purpose for which his soul burned, a cause so just and noble that it drove sleep from him at night, and here he was still unable to pursue it. Obstacle after obstacle had been placed in his path—lately and most notably the task of finding his brother and delivering a message from their father.

Jason scowled. It was his father's ploy, of course, to keep him from his course. But it would serve Robin naught. Jason was determined. Never mind that his course was one his father had forbidden him to pursue and one his former master had counseled him against.

But what else was he to do with himself? His eldest brother, Phillip, had estates aplenty and the burden of someday inheriting their father's title to harrow up his mind and try his soul. His other brother Kendrick burned like a flame, driving himself from conquest to conquest, as if he sought to force a dozen lifetimes into the one he would be allotted. Jason had no stomach for the tidiness of Phillip's life or the incessant roaming of Kendrick's. But he did have the stomach for a bit of crusading. A goodly bit. A bit that might take him out of England for years and give purpose to his life.

That it might also brighten up his reputation was nothing to sneeze at either.

But he sneezed just the same, all over a guardsman, who hastily backed away as if Jason had been spewing curses at him instead of the contents of his nose.

Jason scowled at the man and continued on his way toward the stables. At least his path there was clear—and likely only because his sire hadn't been able to find a way to thwart him so far from home. No doubt he would find more distractions awaiting him in France, should he by any chance find Kendrick, discharge his duty, then sail to the continent before he was too old to hoist a sword. But he would never have the chance to set foot on yonder shore if he didn't finish his business on the current shore, which was, of course, why he found himself chasing the king's court from London north, following his brother's erratic trail, and sleeping in haylofts with inadequate bedding.

The only positive thing to come of his journey so far was that he hadn't found the king at a monastery, as was often his custom. Jason knew he'd have trouble enough with the king's courtiers and whatever clergy he found himself surrounded by without scores of monks trying to exorcise the demons from him as well.

He dismounted in front of the stables and found a cringing stableboy at his side. He handed the lad his reins, knowing that no one would dare abuse his horse or pilfer his saddlebags. He would likely find them in the usual place—well away from any living soul.

Jason looked about him but found no sign of his brother in amongst the horseflesh. Perhaps Kendrick was romping out in the fields with some fair wench, crushing flowers and hearts beneath his heel with equal abandon.

The thought of flowers made his nose begin to twitch, so he decided to leave the fields for a later time and concentrate his search first on the castle itself. He crossed the courtyard and climbed the steps into the great hall.

He made himself known to the highest ranking of Henry's aides present there. The man was a foreigner of indeterminate origin, so Jason tried first French, then Latin. After receiving baffled, unhelpful shrugs in response to both, he gave up and excused himself with a bow. Obviously, he would have to search on his own.

He looked about him but saw no sign of his unruly brother. That meant nothing. Kendrick could have been anywhere, in any guise, stirring up any kind of trouble. That he was even rumored to be at court came as something of a surprise. Kendrick made no secret of his loathing of the king's flaws. Henry had an inordinate fondness for anything or anyone who had not sprung from English soil, and he seemed determined to beggar the country entertaining his entourage and building his monuments in London. Jason could only assume Kendrick was here to flatter the king into giving him, or selling him at a reduced price, some bit of land Kendrick had taken a fancy to.

Either that or Kendrick had been instructed by their father to lead Jason on a merry chase for as long as possible—likely in hopes that Jason would regain his good sense before he rushed off to do something foolish in France.

Damn them both.

Jason considered investigating bedchambers but thought better of it. Interrupting his brother whilst at his favorite labors was more than even he could stomach at present. But a solar might not be so perilous. After all, what havoc could possibly be wreaked in a woman's solar?

Jason climbed the stairs and started down the passageway, looking for a likely door. He hadn't taken a handful of paces before he saw a woman standing outside a door with her head bowed. Her hand was pressed against the wood, as if she couldn't quite bring herself to push the door open. She wasn't a servant; that much he could see by her clothing. Then why did she wait without?

He approached, heralding the like with a mighty sneeze stifled in the crook of his elbow. He dragged his sleeve across his face, immediately relinquishing the idea of making any kind of agreeable impression. He looked at the woman but could not see her very well. The place where she stood was filled with the deepest shadows in the passageway.

"My lady?" he said politely.

She did not lift her bowed head to look at him. She was silent for a moment, then acknowledged him with a soft "my lord."

"Do you require aid?"

"Aid?" she asked. "Nay, my lord, but I thank you for the offer."

Jason approached, then realized that the door was not closed, but rather slightly ajar. He could hear voices inside, and they were passing unpleasant in their tone.

"I could not believe my eyes."

"Nor could I! And the saints only know how long he'd been talking to her yesterday."

"Why would he pass time with her? Nothing could make up for the ugliness of her visage."

"Aye, and not that she had time to lift her skirts—"

"And not that he would have accepted *that* offer, even if he'd kept his eyes closed—"

Another voice spoke, a voice that sent chills down Jason's spine though he had never in his life been frightened by the sound of a woman speaking.

"She must be stopped."

Jason looked at the woman standing next to him. Did they speak of her? All he could see was the top of her head, so he couldn't judge by her expression if that were the case. But he could well imagine her not wanting to go inside and listen to any more of that rot—even if it had naught to do with her.

"Do you require something inside there?" he whispered.

She did not look up, even at that. "I thought to fetch my stitchery, but I daresay there isn't a need for that now."

"No doubt your gear will keep," Jason agreed, fully intending to wish her good fortune, bid her farewell, and then continue his search.

But two things stopped him.

One was that he'd heard his brother's name begin to be bandied about inside the solar. And the second was the woman who stood before him, cloaked in shadows, listening to the drivel being spewed inside that solar as if she needed to hear it. He stood not two paces from her but suddenly felt as if they two stood alone in the world. It was all he could do to breathe normally.

Who was this woman?

She stepped back from the door and pulled the hood of her cloak up around her face. And the moment was gone.

"I thank you for your kindness, my lord," she said. "I'm sure my things will be safe enough."

Jason had his doubts about that, but he also had no desire to enter the solar to find out. He was also beginning to wonder if he might need to break his fast soon. Obviously, he was faint from hunger and from the sneezes that threatened to overwhelm him at every turn. He had no ties to the woman before him. There was no good reason to feel as though the last thing he should do was walk away from her. By the saints, he had no idea what she even looked like! He shook his head to clear it. The sanest thing he could do was turn tail and flee.

Aye, that was wise. But he could not leave her where she was, not with the talk that was going on inside that solar.

"Might I es . . . ah—*ahchoo*—" he said with a mighty sneeze. He dragged his sleeve across his face and tried to regain his dignity. "Might I escort you to wherever you're going?" he said again. Perhaps the sunshine would burn his illness—and his sudden madness—from him before it overcame him completely.

"There's no need," the woman protested.

"My mother would be disappointed in me if I showed such a lack of courtesy," he said. "And who am I to disappoint her?"

"Very well," the woman said with a soft sigh. "But it won't be far. I'm only to go to the barbican gates."

Jason bowed to her, then followed her down the passageway.

"Whom go you to meet?" he asked as they reached the bottom of the stairs.

"No one of consequence," she said, her quiet voice almost lost in the bustle of the hall.

"A handsome knight come to woo you?" he asked lightly.

"I should think not," she said with half a laugh. "Nay, 'tis but a friend I made yesterday in the most unlikely of ways who offered to rescue me from a day passed inside the walls."

And given that her alternative would have been sitting in a solar with a handful of poisonous serpents, he could well understand her desire to accept the deliverance.

They left the great hall and crossed the bailey. Jason tried to steal looks at the woman beside him, but her cloak too thoroughly shadowed her face. He wondered why she chose to go about thusly, especially in the heat of the sun. Perhaps she met a lover for a secret tryst and wanted no one to recognize her. But surely there were few enough people at Henry's temporary court here that she would instantly be known by her clothing and bearing alone.

He shrugged aside his questions, for they weren't vital ones. If she wanted to hide herself, 'twas her affair and not his. What he needed to do was discharge his obligation to her so he could be about his business.

Which was, he thought with a scowl, much like what he was doing with his damned brother he couldn't seem to find.

They walked through the barbican gate. The woman stopped and looked about her. Jason saw her shoulders sag, and immediately sympathy surged through him. Obviously, the invitation hadn't been a trustworthy one. And then he caught sight of a tall figure loitering under a tree some distance down the road.

There was something unsettlingly familiar about that shape, dressed as it was in nun's gear.

"Perhaps there?" Jason said, pointing toward the beginning of an orchard.

The woman paused, then made a sound that Jason could have almost mistaken for a laugh.

"Perhaps," she agreed, and started down the path.

Jason followed, scowling fiercely and cursing under his breath.

The nun straightened as they approached, then walked toward them with a slow and solemn gait.

"My lady," the nun said in a high, hoarse voice. "You came as you said you would."

"Aye," the woman said, sounding amused.

"And I see you've brought your fool with you," the nun said, hiding hairy arms by tucking them into opposite sleeves. "Off with you, dolt. We've a walk to accomplish today."

The woman next to Jason stiffened. Perhaps she thought him offended by the other's words. He wasn't. It wasn't the first time he'd been insulted by the soul before him.

Nor was he surprised to find a nun with a voice that was better suited to bellowing battle cries than chanting prayers. He folded his arms over his chest and glared at the object of his search.

Which was, of course, his brother.

In skirts.

Not that such was all that unusual. Kendrick wasn't the first man in their long and illustrious line to disguise himself as a sister of the cloth. Jason had never in the past—and he prayed fervently that he would never be compelled to in the future—lowered himself to dress as a woman.

Dire circumstances called for momentous actions, he supposed. He wondered what sorts of straits Kendrick found himself in at present to necessitate such a disguise.

Then he found himself distracted by a movement at his side. The woman turned to look at him, and her hood caught on a low branch. It was pulled away to reveal dark hair coiled around her head and a visage that Jason could not look away from.

She was beautiful.

Or at least she had been before the pox.

He smothered his surprise, then gave her his most gentle smile.

"My lady," he said, making her a little bow, "surely you don't intend to pass your afternoon with this oaf here. His mere presence will put you off your food, cause you great pains in the head, and give you horrible dreams. Better that you allow me to save you from this unsavory invitation."

He found himself quite suddenly sprawled on his backside and 'twas a certainty only Kendrick could have put him there.

"Come, Lianna," Kendrick said, offering her his arm. "Let us leave the refuse along the side of the road and be on our way."

"But, my lord—"

"It isn't 'my lord.' It's simply Kendrick. And that unwholesome bit of offal is my younger brother, Jason. He's likely come to torment me with some business I've no stomach for hearing today. See you how the sun shines and the birds sing. We should enjoy it, don't you think?"

Jason thought many things, first and foremost of which was that he really should kill his brother at his earliest opportunity. Perhaps he would invite Kendrick to a war where he could commit fratricide with more ease.

Contemplating that happy possibility was almost enough to get him to his feet with a smile. He rose just the same, brushed off his abused backside, and stared at the ridiculous pair walking away from him. The lady, Lianna, was a mystery he wished he had time to solve. Why did she find herself at court? And what, the saints pity the poor girl, was she doing befriending his randy brother, who could have had any and all of the most beautiful women in England or France tumbling into his bed at the mere hint of an invitation?

He paused, tempted to solve those mysteries.

But nay, he couldn't. He had business to accomplish. The mystery of his brother's whereabouts was solved. Jason had little doubt he could find Kendrick again easily. Only his brother would clothe himself as a nun and stride about with his hairy legs clearly showing under skirts that hit him just below the knee and a cloak that didn't fall to the middle of his forearm—and believe that such a disguise would deceive any but the most foolish of men.

Or women, if that was his purpose, which Jason suspected it might be.

He was momentarily tempted to follow them and force Kendrick to speak with him immediately, but he could already see himself using his fists on his brother, and it would be just his luck to have someone see him brawling with a nun. His reputation was black enough without that.

Nay, he would but wait for supper, then see to delivering his message.

Then he would be on his way to France.

Three

Lianna sat in the shadows and stared at the fire in the midst of the great hall. The smoke burned her eyes if she didn't blink often enough, but such was the price one paid for a roof over one's head, she supposed. In her sire's hall, the fires had been set into the wall, with flues to carry the smoke outside. Her father's people had thought him mad to do such a thing, but he had been convinced of the wisdom of it. And Lianna, her eyes now burning in the midst of the king's appropriated hall, heartily agreed with her sire's thinking.

But at least the smoke gave her a reason to let her eyes water, which they wanted to do just the same from the kindnesses she'd been shown that day.

She peered through the smoke at the king's table and tried to discern the goings-on there. Normally, she would have been sitting there as well, but tonight all the places had been given to lords of either importance or wealth—such as Kendrick of Artane.

Or of dark reputation, given who sat next to Kendrick.

She picked absently at her supper and contemplated the very unlikely turn her life had taken over the past two days. Apparently, giving her tongue free rein in the presence of—and, unfortunately, in the most unflattering ways *about*—one of the most sought-after men in the realm had amused him enough to turn him into something of a comrade-in-arms. She had passed a delightful day in his company, finding him to be nothing that his critics said he was and everything they said he was not. In Artane's second son, she had found a brother and a friend.

Now, *his* brother was a different tale entirely.

From the very moment she had heard Lord Jason's voice in her ear, she'd been unsettled. She'd tried not to show that, to walk as other women did, speak with levity, and carry herself as if she hadn't a care in her heart. She'd certainly had no intention of letting him know what his brief kindness, or the mere sound of his voice in the passageway, had wrought in her. And she'd done her best to forget him as she walked with his brother in the sunlight and heard that brother tell stories of Jason as if he'd been a harmless pup—which Lianna couldn't believe he was.

Not if the rumors were true.

But none of those rumors was foul enough to dissuade her from searching for him through the smoke in the hall and wondering if his visage was as beautiful as she remembered, or if perhaps the spell he'd cast on her had been completely undone by an afternoon passed in his brother's sparkling company. Indeed, she began to suspect that Kendrick had wrought a goodly work on her wits, for she could scarce remember what Jason looked like.

Or so she told herself.

Odd how it had never occurred to her that Kendrick's brother might be even more handsome than he.

But nay, she couldn't say that, for she was just certain she couldn't remember Jason's visage, or the deep whisper of his voice, or the way chills went through her just standing next to him.

She sighed and rested her chin on her fist. Perhaps she was more interested than she cared to admit. And since the hall was smokey enough that he would never see her gaping at him, why shouldn't she? She decided to allow herself that luxury as she peered at him and thought back on what Kendrick had told her.

Jason had been a pleasant, cheerful lad at one time: Kendrick had assured her of such as he'd told her stories of his family. And according to Kendrick, Jason was still cheerful, though Lianna could scarce believe it. Shadows hung about him like shrouds. The current grimness of his visage—what she could see of it from where she sat—warned any and all he would not be amenable to light-hearted conversation. She certainly had no intention of daring the like. Besides, she had just learned to speak freely and comfortably to his brother—and Kendrick was as open as a flower that begged you to come pluck it and savour its fragrance.

Jason of Artane was nightshade, deadly to those who dared partake.

And so beautiful she could scarce convince herself she shouldn't.

She stared at him thoughtfully and began to suspect that perhaps they might have more in common than she wanted to believe. He seemed to have no more stomach for the pleasantries of court than she. She squinted and marked Kendrick laughing with, flattering, and charming the king and his courtiers. She knew that he spoke several languages, for she had heard for herself as he imitated each of the king's foreigners in their own tongues in turn as they walked through the orchard. Those same souls might not have hung on his every word so fully had they but known what amusement Kendrick had had at their expense not a handful of hours before. Even so, there was not a man there at that high table who didn't laugh with

Kendrick or find himself being drawn into the talk.

Except Jason, who put his head down and plowed through his supper with the concentration of a body that hadn't had a decent meal in a fortnight.

And when he did lift his head, he looked bored to tears.

She couldn't help but feel a certain kinship with him in that regard.

"Lady Lianna?"

The voice startled her so badly she almost fell from her chair. She turned around to find Linet of Byford standing beside her, shifting uncomfortably.

"The lady of H-Harrow asks if you w-w-would not be more comfortable in our . . . c-c-circle," Linet said, stumbling badly over her words, "when the entertainments begin." She looked behind her to where Maud had already begun to set up her own little court. As if Maud had arranged it, the king stood and the tables began to be set aside to clear spaces for whatever amusements had been arranged.

Lianna was surprised by the invitation, and she couldn't help but wonder if Kendrick's arrival hadn't heralded more than just an afternoon's freedom from the prison of her visage. If these ladies were deigning to include her as well, who knew what might happen in the ensuing days?

The thought was truly staggering.

"Well," Lianna said, rising, "aye, I daresay I would. Thank you."

Linet looked as miserable as if she'd been banished to the kitchens, and that made Lianna pause. Did that bode ill for her? Was Linet dreading having to spend any more time than necessary in Lianna's company? Then why invite her for the remainder of the eve?

When she reached the circle, the others who waited only wore friendly expressions. A chair was placed on Maud's right, and Lianna was welcomed into it. When she was seated, she was handed a goblet of wine and offered a plate of sweets.

"You must forgive us," Maud said. "We have been less than friendly to you, and for that we are truly sorry. Aren't we, ladies?"

The others bobbed their heads obediently.

Maud looked back at Lianna. "Come, eat," she said, indicating the plate. "Drink. Take your ease with us. There will be fine minstrels to sing to us of heroic deeds. Will that please you?"

Maud smiled and Lianna tried to smile back. But something about Maud's smile disturbed her greatly, for it seemed to fashion itself about her mouth only. No vestige of warmth reached the woman's eyes.

Lianna wished quite suddenly that she'd refused the invitation, but 'twas far too late to leave at present. She looked about her desperately for a place to hide, but found only a wooden plate in one of her hands and a goblet of drink in the other.

So she buried her face in her cup to escape. When she found the brew to be quite nasty, she occupied her hands and her mouth with the sweets until they tasted just as noxious as the other, forcing her to drink more to get them down her throat.

Just as she thought she could bear no more, she looked up to find Kendrick of Artane standing there, frowning down at her thoughtfully.

And behind him, looking as harmless as a clutch of nettles, scowled his younger brother. He glanced at her, then suddenly and quite violently sneezed all over his brother's back.

Kendrick's curse was formidable.

"I need to speak with you," Jason said pointedly. "Turn yourself about."

"Why, so you can drench the front of me? I'll speak with you later. I've more important things to do at present." He made Maud and her companions a bow. "Ladies. My lady," he said, bowing to Lianna as well.

"The dancing begins," Maud said, jumping to her feet

as if she'd been launched there. "My lord, if you will allow me to be so bold?"

Kendrick inclined his head and led Maud off without so much as a murmur of protest, though he exchanged a brief, unpleasant look with his brother on the way by. Jason cursed, swept the women before him with a disgruntled glance, then sat down in Maud's vacated chair. He dragged his sleeve across his watering eyes, then looked with faint interest at Lianna's cup and plate.

"Finished?" he asked.

She had scarce managed an aye before he took the cup and tasted the last drop.

Then he suddenly went very still.

"I'll take that, my lord," said Adela, reaching forward.

Jason did not move. "Will you? I think not. Indeed, I might want some of this myself. Have you any more of this brew?"

"The king's finest," squeaked Linet. "Lady Harrow obtained it for us."

Lianna could not fathom why Jason looked suddenly so angry or why the women about her looked suddenly quite so pale.

Then she realized who sat with them, and his reputation gave her all the answer she needed. He was the Dragon's man, likely something of a dragon himself, and a fit of foul temper had overcome him. No wonder the women about her were so terrified. Indeed, Lianna suspected that she as well should be just as terrified, but somehow she wasn't. She put the plate on the floor and gave Jason her most dazzling smile, only realizing as she looked him full in the face that she shouldn't be doing the like, not with her visage.

But somehow she couldn't find the energy to hide. So she spoke boldly and wondered at her boldness, for it was certainly newfound.

" 'Tis but wine, my lord," she said, then she stopped, for she found that her tongue wasn't working properly.

Indeed, all of the sudden, she felt heartily and thoroughly sick.

"Too much wine," offered Linet.

"I daresay," Jason said darkly.

Lianna pushed herself to her feet, wondering desperately if she might make either the outside or a garderobe before she was violently ill.

"She's going to sick up her supper on my feet," Adela said with distaste. "Go elsewhere, Lianna. These are new slippers I'm wearing."

Lianna felt Jason's hands suddenly on her arms, but she pushed him away. She turned and stumbled toward the stairs, praying she could make the passageway. She could be sick there. But please, just not here in front of the king's company. Not here where she would be fodder for mockery.

She stumbled up the stairs, gained the garderobe by sheer willpower, then hung her head over the hole and wretched until she could scarce stand.

It took a lifetime to retreat to the passageway and several more to walk a handful of paces.

Her head felt as if someone had taken an axe to it, and her poor form no better. And then, quite suddenly, a blessed darkness began to descend.

"Lianna!" a deep voice called urgently from behind her.

But she could not turn, nor could she answer. She closed her eyes and slid happily down the slope toward blackness. The last thing she heard was a mighty sneeze, followed by an equally mighty curse.

She did not feel the arms that broke her fall.

Four

Jason knelt in the passageway with the lady Lianna of somewhere-yet-to-be-discovered in his arms and wondered why in the bloody hell she found herself at court with women who had likely poisoned her.

Perhaps she had no choice, and for that he pitied her. He'd been at Henry's court less than a day, and already he couldn't wait to escape. He couldn't stomach the thought of much more conversation that revolved around the perfect cut of a man's tunic, the proper color for hose, or how one might dress to best grace the latest of the king's building projects. What he wanted was a simple conversation about the feeding of swine, or whether the barley and hops might grow well in the north fields, or a discussion of the virtues of the keep's blacksmith.

Aye, he could scarce wait to take his leave. He would have, and that night, too, had it not been for the woman in his arms.

He'd seen her at supper, hiding in the shadows. He'd

watched her be drawn into the ladies' circle after supper and felt alarm sweep through him. Surely they would have no kindness for such a one as she. He'd followed Kendrick willingly, not only to hound his brother, but also to see what mischief the women were combining.

After his brother had made his nimble escape, Jason had decided to wait him out and keep watch over Lianna whilst he was doing it. Besides, it gave him somewhere to sit where the conversation might revolve around something besides men's garments.

He'd noticed almost immediately that Lianna had looked flushed, and he'd wondered what she'd been drinking. Tasting her wine had assured him 'twas more than simply the brew that had worked such a foul business on her.

And now, as he stared down into her poor, ravaged face, he could only hope she didn't pay the ultimate price for having trusted those who had given it to her.

Women Jason would see repaid for their misdeed, in time.

He dragged his arm across his running nose then swung Lianna up into his arms. He kicked at the first door he saw. It was opened none too quickly by a sleepy servant.

"Let me in," Jason growled.

"But, my lord," the woman squeaked, "this is the ladies' chamber. You cannot—"

"I can and I will," Jason said. He pushed past her, strode across the chamber, and jerked back the bedcurtains. He laid Lianna down and wondered if he shouldn't undress her as well. Her gown was soiled and would likely be better off in some pile of rags destined for the beggars.

He looked at the servants huddled behind him and chose the one who looked the least likely to harm Lianna further.

"Strip her," he commanded, "and dress her in clothing

she can wear abed comfortably. I will wait without." He looked at the other two servants. "Leave."

"But, my lord," protested one.

He merely gestured curtly toward the door, and the women quit the chamber without further comment. Jason followed them out, then pulled the door shut behind him. He leaned back against it and stared grimly at the wall facing him. Now that he had peace for thinking, he would have to decide on a course of action. He could only hope that Lianna had managed to vomit up all but the quickest of the poison.

He had just begun to consider what he might give her to aid her when he noticed a commotion to his left. There coming toward him were the women responsible for Lianna's distress, trailed by the servants he had tossed from the chamber. Jason simply could not believe they had innocently given her drink laced with death. Worse still was how they walked about so freely, as if they thought no one would think to question their actions.

"Move yourself," one woman said briskly. "And take that foolish girl inside with you. I'm certain her illness is but a ruse."

"What was in her wine?" Jason asked.

One of the other women made a sound of misery and slumped back against the wall. That was telling enough, he supposed.

"Something in her wine, my lord?" the first woman said evenly. "How could you think such a thing of us?"

Jason looked at the woman who faced him with such apparent lack of fear, and suddenly a name attached itself to the face. Maud of Harrow, who possessed a tongue more poisonous than an adder's. He should have known she would have been behind this.

"I have eyes," he said, "and I recognize the signs."

"Having brewed several unwholesome things yourself," the lady of Harrow said with a cold smile. "Along with casting spells and other such activities particular to your kind."

"Or so it is rumored," one of the other women agreed.

"Silence, Adela," Maud commanded. She turned back to Jason and smiled unpleasantly at him.

"I have many skills," he said with a shrug, silently marveling that she would so boldly accuse him of sorcery. "I daresay you wouldn't want to acquaint yourself with too many of them."

"You don't frighten me," Maud said, puffing herself up.

But it would seem that he frightened the rest of her rabbits, for the other three were near to collapse in the passageway.

"Perhaps I don't," Jason conceded. "But you don't know the extent of what I can do. Especially my talent for carrying tales to the king to ruin the lives of foolish, spiteful wenches possessing sharp tongues and few wits. Do you care for a performance of that one?"

Maud considered, then turned and, one by one, slapped three whimpering women smartly across their faces.

"On your feet, Linet. Come, Adela. Stand up, Janet, you fool! Let us be away. We'll sleep in the solar."

Jason waited, faintly satisfied, until they had stomped away before he turned and went back inside the chamber. The serving girl was covering Lianna with blankets.

But Lianna wasn't moving.

Jason hastened to the side of the bed. The servant looked up as he approached.

"I did as ye bid me, milord," she said. "But she's powerful ill."

"Aye," Jason said absently. "I daresay 'twas poison."

"Mayhap 'tis mostly gone from her."

"Let us pray that 'tis so," he said. "Fetch my brother, will you? I've an errand for him. I'll need several things from the healer, if the man can provide them."

"Aye, milord, as ye will."

Jason sent the woman on her way, then looked about

him for something to sit on. Finding a small stool, he pulled it near the bed, sat, and searched back through his own lessons at a healer's knee for what he should do at present. His lessons had been thorough, and most unusual, given from whom he'd had them. He smiled to himself at the thought. Perhaps the lady of Harrow had not spoken amiss after all. He could brew a love potion, cure warts and other afflictions, and slather on quite a salve of beauty, should circumstances require.

As well as spew out a variety of quite potent curses, which was enormously tempting at the moment.

But the saints pity him should he not be able to remember the simple herbs to aid the woman before him in ridding her body of what foul brew she'd ingested.

He contemplated that list of herbs for what seemed to him an inordinately long amount of time. He was on the verge of going to seek out Kendrick himself when the door opened and a torch entered the chamber, carried by none other than his yawning brother.

"Lianna, where are you? I know that to have called me to you as I was about to retire can only mean that you've one desire of me—"

Kendrick's yawn ceased abruptly when he saw who was laid out on the bed.

"What happened to her?" he said, coming to stand next to Jason.

"To Lianna?" Jason asked, looking up at his brother sourly. "To the woman you couldn't see fit to introduce to me?"

Kendrick looked at him blankly. "I was tormenting you. 'Tis my sworn duty as your elder brother to do so. Now, what happened to her? She was seemingly happy enough with the ladies. When I was summoned here, I thought perhaps she had a tryst in mind."

"With you? Poor girl, I should hope not," Jason said.

"Why not? Many women—"

"Aye, exactly. Perhaps this one has more sense than the others."

Kendrick flicked him smartly on the ear, then peered over his shoulder. "Why are you here then? And see you how she sleeps. What have you done, Jason? Bored her so deeply that she must sleep to escape you?"

"Kendrick, you fool, she was poisoned!"

Kendrick gasped. "Nay! By whom?"

"By those who would have you, likely."

"Stupid wenches. Surely no man is worth this—not even I."

At least in that his brother was showing some sense. Jason reached for Lianna's hand and held it between his own. Her flesh felt as if it were on fire. Jason looked up at his brother.

"Go fetch me herbs," he said.

Kendrick blinked. "Are you brewing love potions for her now?"

"Healing ones, dolt."

"One never knows, what with your teachers."

"Berengaria is a fine healer."

"Oh, aye," Kendrick agreed, "she is that. I daresay her two accomplices might have a different tale to tell about her varied talents and whether or not she is of the witchly ilk. Though I must admit Phillip was no worse for the wear for his time spent in their company."

Phillip, their older brother, had followed his bride on a merry chase, accompanied by none other than Berengaria of Artane, lately of Blackmour, and her two apprentices, one of whom had willingly gone north in search for—of course—the thumb-bone of a wizard.

Whether she had found it or not was something of a family secret.

Jason smiled faintly. "They were all that aided him in taming his bride, so I daresay he has no complaints. And now that you've convinced yourself my skills aren't dark ones, go fetch me what I need."

"I'm not at all sure your skills aren't dark ones," Kendrick said with half a laugh, "but I will fetch you what you require, then I will return and make certain that our lady's honor isn't compromised by having you loitering about her chamber alone with your own sour self."

Jason spat out his list at his brother, then rose and gave him a healthy shove toward the door.

"Shall I bring you anything else?" Kendrick asked from the doorway. "Something for your sneezes? Or can you spell yourself into good health?"

"Horehound," Jason said shortly. "It will serve me as well as the lady here. But be swift, for I would waste no more time in seeing to the rest of this poison."

"As you will," Kendrick said, turning to leave.

"And a lute," Jason added.

"Lute?" Kendrick echoed. "And where am I to find—"

"There are musicians aplenty. Filch one of theirs."

Kendrick sighed and left without further comment.

Jason stared after him and spared a fleeting thought for how he really should be following his brother out that door, down the stairs, and out the castle gates. He had a crusade to make, kings to woo, and a noble cause to righteously pursue.

None of which had anything to do with where he was at present or what poor service he felt compelled to render here.

Jason sat, bowed his head over Lianna's hand, and offered up the most humble prayer his black soul could muster. His other life would have to wait while he fought for this life here. He could only hope he had enough skill to save that life.

With the way she was breathing so unevenly, he wasn't sure he would manage it.

Five

Lianna was sure she had died.

And by the sound of things, she was certain, though somewhat surprised, that she had actually been admitted straight to Heaven without having to spend any time doing penance in Purgatory.

Music surrounded her, music that sounded remarkably like that made by a lute. That was puzzling, to be sure, as she'd always been led to believe that choirs of angels would attend the entrance of any soul through those Eternal Gates. But perhaps she was lowly enough—and had barely sufficed as an entrant—to merit naught but a single instrument to welcome her home.

And then the chord went astray.

"Damn."

Lianna struggled to open her eyes. Perhaps she'd sinned more than she thought to merit naught but a lute and a lutenist who dared curse in such a place. Perhaps she was still on the outskirts of the Eternal City, trapped with those who were still seeking to make themselves presentable.

"You should have practiced more," said a deep voice.

Lianna did manage to open her eyes then, though the sight that greeted her was no less baffling than what she'd imagined.

"I did practice. I practiced a great deal. Father vowed the sweet sounds of a lute were the way to win a lady's heart. I practiced until my bloody fingers were bloody!"

"In between consorting with witches, warlocks, and other sorcerers of dubious origins, of course."

"Aye, well, that too."

Lianna blinked. She would have rubbed her eyes as well, but her hands were too heavy to lift. She looked blearily at the two great birds sitting not far from her, one with fair feathers and one with dark. The dark bird was tall and graceful, with a proud tilt to his head and shining dark eyes. He was also holding the lute and cursing now and again. The fair bird next to him opened his beak and snorted.

Did winged creatures snort? She puzzled that out for several moments, but could come to no useful decision on it.

"It isn't as if *you* practiced any," the lute-playing one grumbled.

"And as you might imagine, my bed has not suffered from my lack of it. You must have more than pitiful skills on a lute to keep and hold the attention of a woman, brother."

"I have more skills than that."

"As one sees from the flocks of women who fight each other to have you."

Flocks of women? He obviously meant flocks of female birds. Lianna struggled to make sense of what they said, but it was difficult. She listened to them toss insults at each other, with increasingly unpleasant curses attached, for quite some time before it occurred to her that fowl such as these were certainly not members of any angelic choir, nor were they likely to be accompanying that choir anytime soon. A slow, steady feeling of terror swept over her.

"Nay," she breathed, when she could manage to find the word.

The dark bird immediately fastened a piercing gaze upon her hapless self, as if he intended to make a meal of her.

She tried to focus on him, but he seemed to weave about greatly, as if either he could not remain still or she could not. After trying to divine the truth of it for several minutes, she gave herself over to the only truth she knew.

She hadn't gone to Heaven. Heaven could not produce lute-playing birds with such foul speech. There was only one place for such as she, and she had apparently traveled there without delay. She felt tears begin to slip down her cheeks.

"I've gone to Hell," she wept.

"What?" the dark one asked.

"Foul notes, foul words," she managed.

And at that, the fair-feathered bird tossed back his head, opened his beak, and roared out a laugh.

She watched as the dark bird reached out toward her. No doubt he intended to clutch her with that hand he had suddenly fashioned himself and carry her down with him to his fiery dungeon. The saints pity her, she was doomed.

Blackness engulfed her, and she knew no more.

She woke, only realizing then that she had been asleep. She stirred, and her poor form set up such a clamor that she immediately ceased all movement save drawing in hesitant breaths. By the saints, what had befallen her? Had someone beaten her nigh onto death?

She lay still for several minutes, searching back through her memories for one of any sense. There were dreams aplenty, ones with large birds and rather pleasant strumming of a lute, but those were surely naught but madness. Had she been ill? She had very vivid memories of the pox and how her fever had raged. This was akin to that but somehow worse, as if every part of her had been assaulted by some foul thing.

She could make out the bedhangings above her. Heavy layers of blankets and furs covered her. She was abed, which was something in itself given that she'd passed the majority of her nights as a member of the king's entourage sleeping on a straw pallet on the floor. The chamber was light, but that was from daylight, not candlelight. She turned her head to the right, wondering if she might be able to see out the window. But what she found was enough to still her forever.

Jason of Artane sat on a stool not a handful of paces away.

He was leaning back against the wall, his head tipped to one side, sound asleep. Lianna could scarce believe her eyes. How had he found his way into her chamber? And what, by all the blessed saints of Heaven, was he doing sleeping here? She looked to his right to find a serving maid curled up on the floor, sound asleep as well. Interesting though that might have been, it surely did not merit any further notice. So she turned her attentions back to the man who slept sitting up on a stool, with his hands limp in his lap and his mouth open to admit the passage of a soft snore or two.

He was almost close enough for her to touch him.

Deadly nightshade that he was.

But he didn't look deadly at present. He looked innocent and harmless and at peace. He looked like a man who would draw a child onto his lap and tell it stories for the whole of the afternoon if asked. He looked like a man who would pull his lady wife into his arms, rest his chin atop her head, and tell her he was happy to face life with her beside him. He looked like the sort of man her father would have found no fault with.

He looked like a man on the verge of drooling.

That sort of catastrophe was seemingly enough to rouse him from slumber, for he straightened with a snort, smacked his lips a time or two, then opened his eyes. And a smile of such dazzling brightness crossed his features, she was near blinded by it.

And at that moment, she was firmly and irretrievably lost.

He dropped to his knees at her bedside. "The saints be praised," he said, looking at her with visible relief. "Can you speak?"

She swallowed. "Aye," she whispered.

He put his hand to her forehead, and she received another pleased smile as a result.

"Your fever is but a slight one, though I daresay you're still recovering from the fierce one you've already had." Then he looked at her and frowned. "Do you know who I am?"

"Jason de Piaget."

"Well done, though we certainly cannot thank my brother for an introduction. And you're the lady Lianna, though you needn't thank my brother for that either, for he was very closemouthed about you. I had to pry all I know of you from the servants."

She could only imagine what he'd heard. She managed a snort of disgust.

"Nay, my lady, they were very few, those tales, and surely pleasant enough," he said with another smile. "Now, tell me how you fair. Shall you have a drink? I daresay food is beyond you still, but a bit of watered-down wine might suit." He looked toward the servant. "Aldith?"

The servant sat up sleepily and rubbed her eyes. When she saw Lianna awake, she rose to her knees.

"The saints be praised."

"Aye," Jason agreed. "Fetch a bit of the king's finest, won't you, and water to go with it. If anyone forbids you, tell them I commanded it and they'll answer to me if they deny you."

"Aye, my lord," she said, and quickly rose to her feet and left the chamber.

Lianna watched him turn back toward her, and she could scarce believe that Jason of Artane, master of dark arts and other sundry unsavoury habits, was kneeling by her head and now reaching for her hand to hold it between his own.

Odder still that she had no desire to flee in terror.

Indeed, looking at his beautiful blue eyes and even more pleasing visage, she wondered why anyone would find him anything but a harmless pup.

"The wine will come," he said confidently.

She managed a smile. "You are unused to being gainsaid, I suppose."

"What is the use of a foul reputation if it serves you nothing?" He looked down at her hand. "You're trembling. I daresay you'll be weak for some time."

"What befell me? Was I beaten?"

He looked at her quickly, one eyebrow raised in surprise. "Beaten? Nay. Poisoned, rather."

"Poisoned?" she breathed.

"The wine you drank. I would imagine your solar companions were ill-pleased with the time you passed with Kendrick."

She thought back. "I remember having a very sour stomach."

"Aye, well, best to forget that night," he said, patting her hand. "You were gravely ill, and I feared the worst. The following days were little better."

It took a moment or two to realize what he had been telling her. Had he stayed with her the entire time? She looked at his face and noted several days' growth of beard there. How many days had it been? Vividly her dream of the two birds came back to her. Had those been Jason and Kendrick, keeping watch by her bed?

And then an even more horrifying thought occurred to her, one that made her turn her head away from Jason in shame.

He had seen her visage. Not only had he looked on it whilst she dreamed, he had been forced to gaze at it whilst she spoke to him as boldly as a harlot. She reached up with the hand he was not holding and pulled some of her hair over her face.

"Thank you, my lord," she said, and her voice sounded horribly choked, even to her ears. "I don't know how I can repay you for your aid."

He said nothing.

She could not bear to look at him to see how he reacted to her words. All she could do was pull her hand free of his and turn more fully away from him.

"I daresay I'm well enough now. You needn't stay any longer. Surely a servant can tend me."

He was silent. Indeed, he was silent for so long, she wondered if he were struggling to master his disgust before he quit the chamber. But she heard no movement. In truth, she could hear nothing but shame pounding in her ears. How bold she had been! More the fool was she.

Then he cleared his throat. "Do you, my lady, know of my former master?"

She frowned. Why ask such a foolish question? Who didn't know of him? Christopher of Blackmour had the very blackest of reputations, full of violence and evil. He could change his shape, weave foul spells, do all manner of things she had never wanted to hear about after the sun went down. He was a dragon who caught unwary travelers in his claws when he wasn't loping over his land in the shape of a ferocious wolf, devouring all who dared set foot on his soil.

And Jason of Artane had been his squire.

The saints only knew what he had learned at his master's knee.

"Aye," she managed finally. "I know of him."

"Well, if you knew him as I do, then you would judge me differently," he said.

She could only imagine how.

"Now, I will go, if you wish it, but I will not go unless you look me in the face and tell me to."

Ah, what kind of man was he to be so cruel? Had Blackmour taught him that as well? She could only shake her head in misery.

He was silent for a goodly while, then spoke again.

"Why do you hide your face?" he asked gently.

"Why do you think?" she cried out, then bit her tongue.

"Do you think me so poor a man as that?" he asked quietly. "So weak-minded? So vain? So hollow in my character that I look only for perfection? Obviously, you have confused me with my brother."

She couldn't stop a smile at that, but neither could she face him.

"If you knew my master as I do, you would realize that he made me into a man who judges not by the sight of his eyes, but rather one who has learned to look deeper and trust what his heart tells him. Now, you do not know me, and you have unfortunately passed already too much time with my cocksure sibling and must, therefore, be permitted a bit of doubt about my character given what you've seen of his. I must tell you, though, that I cannot leave—nay, I will not leave—until you look me full in the face and tell me to go."

It was the hardest thing she had ever done. Indeed, it took more courage than facing the king's company at dinner. It took more courage than passing hours in a solar, closeted with women who loathed her. It took almost as much courage as it had taken to press on after her parents had died. Indeed, she suspected it might require more, for 'twas not her past that she faced.

It was her future.

She couldn't have said why that thought had come to her, but the truth of it burned within her breast. It was the same feeling that had fair set her on fire the first time she'd heard Jason's voice in her ear. It was the feeling that she was facing her destiny.

If she could face him, that is.

So she took a deep breath, brushed the hair back from her face, and turned to look at him.

She couldn't see him, of course. Her eyes were too full of tears.

"Stay or go?" he asked neutrally.

Ah, but that was too much to ask. How could she bid him stay when it might be against his will? She shook her head.

"That was unfair, I suppose," he conceded. "Let me ask it thusly: I wish to stay, though perhaps you might wish me to leave and at least change the clothes I've been wearing for the past several days. I will only go if you cannot bear my presence any longer. Now, shall I stay?"

She was having trouble enough just looking at him without giving in to the almost overwhelming desire to hide her face. But she supposed he would kneel there all day until she gave him some kind of answer, and there was only one answer she could possibly give. So she took what courage was left to her—and it seemed to be increasing by the moment—and cleared her throat.

"Stay," she said, and she was almost surprised by the firmness in her tone.

He smiled and inclined his head. "As my lady wishes. Shall I play for you as well? Whilst we await your wine?"

"Aye," she said.

He hadn't but set fingers to the strings before the door burst open and Kendrick bounded into the chamber, his smile almost blinding in its sunniness.

"Ah, Lianna," he said, beaming down at her, "you're

awake! And none too soon. The saints only know what sorts of frightening sounds Jason has subjected you to whilst you slept. Actually, I was here to hear them, and I would not be lying to tell you they were foul ones indeed." He sat himself down on Jason's lap, completely obscuring his brother from her view. "You look much improved."

"Aye, I am," she croaked.

"Jason is too, if you'll notice. No more sneezing. But the spells he had to cast! The brews he brewed! 'Tis enough to leave any sensible soul trembling—"

Jason reached around and set his lute upon Lianna. "Hold that for me will you, lady? I have this large lump of refuse to remove from your chamber."

She watched in fascination as the brothers engaged in a friendly tussle, which became less friendly after but a moment or two, then seemed to escalate into an all-out war.

"Excuse us—*oof*," Jason said as he doubled over with Kendrick's fist in his belly.

"I'll return brief—*aargh*," Kendrick said as he was propelled out the door thanks to Jason's hands at his throat.

They did pause in the doorway long enough to taste wine that Aldith had brought, then waved her inside and continued their exercises. Aldith crossed the chamber and smiled at Lianna.

"Ye're lookin' well, milady," she said. "And with two such handsome men to attend ye, how could ye not?"

How indeed, Lianna thought, bemused.

But even as she enjoyed that thought, she couldn't help but wonder in the back of her mind just who it had been to give her poison and why.

Six

Jason walked along the passageway and wondered, as ser-vants scattered before him like leaves before a strong wind, if there ever might come a time in his life where he could walk about without frightening everyone he met. Then again, it might serve him. He could be quite an asset on the battlefield. All he would need do was have a herald call out his name and watch the enemy disappear. Surely the king might have a use for him thusly.

But such service would have taken him far from where he wanted to be. He paused before Lianna's door and bowed his head, resting his palm against the wood. That he remained at court of his own will was startling enough. That his noble crusade was seeming less noble and more foolish by the moment was what had driven him to leave a sleeping Lianna's side and pace about the inner bailey, trying to find either his reason or his wits.

Neither of which he seemed to possess any longer.

But when the door opened before him and a very unsteady, though garbed for walking, Lianna of a place no one would tell him stood there clutching the doorway for support, he thought that perhaps his wits and reason hadn't left him after all.

Staying at this woman's side seemed the wisest thing he'd ever contemplated doing.

And he was almost certain his father and his former master would have approved.

"Where go you?" he asked, suppressing the urge to pick her up and carry her back to bed before she could answer.

"To seek my stitchery," she said weakly. "I can lie abed no longer."

Jason frowned. "Surely you've no desire to sit and sew amongst such women as those."

She was silent for a moment, then she lifted her face and looked at him. "What would you have me do else, my lord? I cannot ever hide from them. If it is not them I must endure, it will be others like them."

Jason doubted she could find four more vicious women to subject herself to, but he refrained from saying so. For one thing, she was looking at him without hiding her visage. For another, she was standing there without a hooded cloak around her shoulders for use in hiding later. If she had found the courage to allow the court to see her and not shrink, who was he to gainsay her?

He stepped back a pace and made her a low bow. "As my lady wishes."

She was still too weak to be up. Jason watched her struggle for only a handful of paces before he put his arm around her and gave her little choice but to lean on him. Their pace was very slow. It gave him ample time to wonder if there was a way he could convince her to let him fetch her things. Surely she could sew just as well whilst she was abed.

When they reached the solar door, Lianna straightened. Jason let his arm fall away from her, but he did so reluctantly.

"Are you certain?" he asked softly. "Perhaps another day—"

She shook her head. "I am well enough." Then she looked at him and smiled faintly. "Thank you, my lord. For all your kindnesses to me."

"Jason," he said. "My name is Jason."

"Jason, then," she said, after only a slight hesitation.

"I'll wait for you here."

"But—"

"I'll wait for you here," he said, folding his arms over his chest. "And don't drink any of their bloody brews."

"Far better to drink yours?"

"The worst mine might do is make you fall in love with me," he said, fully meaning for it to come out teasingly, but somehow the words came out of his mouth and hung in the air, still. He stared down at Lianna and couldn't believe that he had revealed so much of his heart with a simple handful of words.

Or that such words had uncovered so much of his heart he hadn't yet been able to face.

She only stared at him for a moment or two in complete silence, then shut her mouth and struggled visibly to look unconcerned.

Jason took a deep breath. "I will," he said, trying desperately for a much lighter tone, "remain without should you need me."

"I vow I won't drink anything."

"Very wise."

She gave him the briefest of smiles before she turned and pushed her way unsteadily into the solar. Jason heard the conversation come to an abrupt halt. The feeling of malice that flowed from the chamber was enough to set his hair on end—and he was the one supposedly accustomed to consorting with all manner of evil-doers.

He immediately tossed aside his promise to remain out in the passageway. He pushed the door fully open, then leaned against the doorframe, where he had full view of the goings-on inside.

Maud of Harrow and her accomplices sat in a circle with their feet at a brazier like so many witches hovering over a pot of bubbling mixture destined to wreak havoc on some unsuspecting soul. Only they weren't watching their feet or their imaginary pot. Their eyes, to a woman, were trained upon Lianna.

And their glances were not friendly ones.

Well, all except Linet of Byford, who Jason had encountered more than once hovering by Lianna's door as if doing penance for her part in the tragedy.

"What are you doing here?" Maud said, her voice as quiet as a knife sliding between unresisting ribs.

"I came to fetch my stitchery," Lianna said, her words steady and sure.

Jason noted her change of plans, but he had no intentions of commenting on it. Even he would have found little to recommend an afternoon in the company of these women.

"Of course," Maud said, gesturing toward the corner with a smile an assassin would have been happy to call his own. "By all means, fetch it."

Lianna made her way carefully across the chamber and knelt down before a small trunk. Jason watched the other women and wondered at the tangible sense of anticipation that seemed to run through them. Had they some new barb to throw at Lianna before she quit the chamber? Surely they wouldn't dare with him standing right there.

And then he realized that Lianna was not moving. He looked over to find her kneeling before her trunk, still as stone.

A feeling of dread swept over him.

He pushed away from the wall, skirted the chairs, and crossed the little chamber to kneel down at Lianna's side. A very hasty look revealed things that would never be useful again. He reached out and lifted up threads that were none of them a quarter the length of his smallest finger. Needles were bent double, past ever being used again for their original purpose. Cloth was torn into strips. He fingered several of those tattered strips and could see that they had once been a tapestry in the making.

And on the top of all the destruction was a charred bit of wood that he could only assume had once been her tapestry frame. The rest had no doubt gone to feed some fire or other.

He wondered why it was that Lianna didn't break down and weep.

He watched as she gently pushed his hand aside, then dug through the ruins of her art. She pulled out a needle. It was bent, but not so thoroughly that it couldn't be saved. Jason watched Lianna finger it for several moments in silence. Then she looked up at him.

And to his surprise, one corner of her mouth seemed to be tipping up, as if it considered beginning a smile.

"They missed something," she remarked calmly.

Indeed, she spoke so calmly they might have been discussing something as unimportant as whether or not the garrison was exercising until past noon or before.

Jason swallowed past a very dry throat. "Did they?" he managed.

Lianna toyed with the needle for a moment or two, then held it up to the light. "Can you brew potions, Jason?"

He blinked in surprise. "I beg your pardon?"

She fixed him with a purposeful glance. "Potions, my lord. Can you brew them?"

He wondered if anything he might say could possibly lead to anything but him being carried off to some unwholesome dungeon and subsequently being put to death in an unpleasant way. But he also suspected he knew what Lianna was thinking, so he stroked his chin, as if he considered his answer.

"Aye," he said finally. "I've been trained to do the like."

Lianna stood, swayed, then steadied herself. She shuffled slowly over to where Linet sat, quivering, all amusement, however faint, gone from her expression.

"Could you brew a potion that would bring death?" Lianna asked.

"Aye, likely so."

Lianna moved to stand behind another woman. "This is the lady Adela. Could you brew up something to ruin whatever wits might remain her?"

"Surely."

She moved behind another woman. "Here is her sister, Janet, a woman of particular desires. Could you see to it that she rots from the inside out, that a man never wanted to lie with her again?"

He suspected Janet would acquire that particular affliction on her own soon enough, but there was no sense in ruining Lianna's play.

"Easily done."

Lianna moved to stand behind Maud of Harrow. Maud sat as stiff as a pillar on her chair, every muscle tensed, a look of absolute hatred on her face.

"What about," Lianna said quietly, "something to ruin a face? To ruin beauty? To take away the visage a woman holds most dear?"

"I could have caught the pox from you and done that," Maud snapped.

"Aye, but that would have been over and done with in a handful of weeks," Lianna said, leaning down close to Maud's ear. "I daresay my lord could find a way to ruin your visage over the course of months, leaving you ample time to mourn your loss." She looked at Jason. "Your thoughts, my lord?"

He lifted his eyebrows. "It could be done. And there could be a great amount of pain with it. Would that please you, my lady?"

Lianna paused, as if she considered, then she straightened and shrugged. "Why trouble yourself? Life will do it to her in time anyway. A woman cannot be so ugly on the inside and not have it seep out eventually. What think you?"

What he thought was that she was the most amazing woman he had ever met and he would be damned lucky if he could ever call her his.

Something he was finding he wanted very much indeed.

And then Maud moved.

Jason was on his feet, across the chamber, and standing between Maud and Lianna before Maud could get to her feet and whirl around to slap Lianna. Jason stared at Maud's upraised hand.

"Lianna," he said, "quit the chamber. I'll fetch your things and follow you."

He held Maud's gaze in the same way he'd held countless opponents, waiting for a twitch in her face or a blink of her eye that would signal her intent to strike first.

She dropped her hand, huffed disdainfully, then spun back around and flung herself down into her chair. Jason waited until Lianna was standing outside the door before he fetched her little trunk, then walked to the door himself. He looked back at the women seated there, then held each of their gazes in turn.

"I sincerely hope," he said quietly, "that you all reap the rewards of what you've sown."

And with that, he left the chamber and closed the door behind him.

Lianna was waiting for him, trembling. He smiled down at her.

"You were extraordinary," he said. "And I'm very sorry about your gear."

She laughed, a choked sound that seemed to go quite well with the tears coursing down her cheeks.

"Aye, well, when compared to the pox or poison, this seems a small thing." She paused. "I am glad you were there."

"You just wanted me for my foul reputation."

"It seemed a pity not to make use of it."

"I daresay there is more to you than meets the eye."

He was just giving thought to how he might go about discovering what that more was when he looked up and saw the very last person he wanted to see at present. He cursed under his breath. Kendrick's ability to ruin any and all of Jason's attempts at wooing a woman was nothing short of uncanny. Did his father have a hand in this as well? Jason glared at his brother.

"What do you want?"

Kendrick blinked innocently. "What mean you?"

"We're busy, as you can see. Be off with you."

Kendrick looked at him assessingly, as if he knew what Jason was planning.

"I thought," Kendrick said slowly, as if he considered something of deep import, "that you had business to be about. Crusading or some such rot."

Jason sensed Lianna looking up at him. He wondered what she would think if he took his fist and planted it solidly in his brother's mouth to stop any more witless words. At least he could do so now and have it accomplish something. He remembered vividly all the years he'd wanted to but couldn't.

"I've changed my mind," Jason growled.

"Ah," Kendrick said wisely. "You found something, well, *here* to change your mind, hmmm?"

"Shut up," Jason said. "Before you force me to see to that for you."

Kendrick looked as if he planned to say something else. Jason brushed past him, nodding to Lianna to come with him. He saw her inside her chamber and set her trunk down by the bed.

"We will seek out a fair and find you other things to stitch with. Or perhaps the king has a stitcher with thread and cloth to spare."

"His Majesty seems to have an abundance of clothing," she agreed.

"I will see what I can find, then return. Does that suit you?"

She sat down on the bed and looked up at him with a smile. "And I've no doubt you've business with your brother."

"You see too clearly," he said with a scowl. "Aye, I'll see to him, find things for you, then return." *And I'll find a guard for your door,* he added silently. He nodded to Lianna, left the chamber, closed the door, then rewarded his brother with a blow to the belly that should have silenced him for a goodly while.

Kendrick straightened with a grunt. "What was that for?"

"I'm thinking to woo her, you fool. I do not need your aid."

Kendrick grunted. "If she'll have you."

"Why wouldn't she?"

"Why indeed?"

"There's nothing amiss with me."

To his surprise, Kendrick clapped him with a friendly hand on the shoulder.

"To be sure, brother. But don't you realize who she is?"

"I was just in the process of trying to discover more about her," Jason said pointedly, "when you arrived with your bothersome self."

"Or what she's doing in the king's company?" Kendrick continued, as if he hadn't heard the slur.

Jason considered briefly, then shook his head. "She's not his lover. She couldn't be."

"She's his ward, dolt."

Jason blinked. "His ward?"

"Aye. She's Lianna of Grasleigh. Didn't you know?"

Grasleigh. *Grasleigh?* Jason felt the blood drain from his face. He remembered well hearing of Grasleigh's death, but he hadn't stopped to consider the daughter who had been left behind after the family's slaughter. And what a daughter—one who possessed almost as much wealth as his sire himself.

"You'll have trouble with the king," Kendrick said unhelpfully. "Doubt he'll want a third son for such as she."

Jason doubted it as well. He leaned back against the wall, wondering why he hadn't been quick enough to have found out who she was before Kendrick did him the honor of informing him.

Kendrick punched his arm. "Cheer up. We'll think of something."

"Thank you," Jason said faintly. "I think."

Kendrick laughed. "Your lack of faith in me wounds me. And when did you fall for her? I thought you were off to pursue your noble cause in France. Though I can understand why you would want her. She is quite remarkable."

"And she doesn't want you."

"You don't know that," Kendrick said with a glint in his eye.

Jason sensed a battle in the offing. At least that might take his mind off the devastating tidings he'd just received.

"She has two eyes," Jason said. "And a nose."

Well, that was enough to do it, Jason found. And as he brawled with his brother in the passageway, he considered how it was he might attain the impossible.

Such as a third son wedding with the richest heiress in England.

Seven

Lianna sat in a comfortable chair under a tree, enjoying the sunshine and poking through the basket of thread Jason had amassed for her over the past three days. At first she'd been too grateful to complain about the colors. Now, she had begun to suspect he'd chosen them with great care.

For they were mostly cheerful colors.

Not the colors of shadows.

Indeed, she suspected that fashioning a shadow or a dragon or anything else gloomy or grim with any of these things would be quite impossible. And that was enough to bring yet another smile to her lips, something that seemed to be happening with alarming regularity.

Especially since she wondered how such happiness could possibly last.

She looked at her companion, who sat on the ground with his back against the tree, plucking the strings of his filched lute and frowning over his fingerings. His blackened eye was healing nicely, and the cut on his lip had scabbed over well enough. She had thought to ask how he'd come by such injuries, but she'd already known the answer—given that she'd listened to him scuffle with his brother in the passageway. And she'd seen Kendrick's face later that day as well.

"You must have an interesting family," she said dryly.

Jason looked up. "Why do you say that?"

"The displays of brotherly affection I've seen between you and Kendrick. Remarkable, truly."

Jason shook his head with a smile. "We love each other well enough, I suppose. What you don't understand is that I've been the youngest all my life, and therefore the one least likely to come out the winner in any conflict."

"Do you all go about bloodying each other's noses regularly?"

"We're wrestling, my lady," he said solemnly. "Harmless encounters. And as I was saying, I always used to come out on the bottom of such friendly skirmishes."

"And then you grew."

"I grew," he agreed. "And my brothers grew fat and lazy. You can imagine why the temptation to best them now at every opportunity is almost overwhelming."

"Kendrick does not seem overplump to me. Has your other brother gone to fat?"

"Gone to seed is more like it," Jason said with a snort. "Nay, Phillip is not fat either, though he's become somewhat less tidy than he used to be. He used to shun wrestling for fear of mussing his clothes." Jason strummed thoughtfully. "I suppose that he's since worn enough of his children's meals to no longer care about the condition of his tunics. Happily for me," he said, looking up at her with twinkling eyes, "such slovenliness and weariness leave him ripe pickings for being vanquished. And Kendrick can be distracted with insults, leaving him vulnerable as well."

"Not that you need to rely on such tactics, of course," she said. "Being so intimidating yourself."

"What with my reputation and all," he agreed.

She nodded but found herself quite abruptly unable to speak further. Thinking on Jason and his brothers and what closeness they shared made her think on things she hadn't in months. A horrible longing for her family rose up and washed over her, a yearning so strong that all she could do was bow her head and bury it in her threads. A tear slid down her cheek and dripped onto her hand.

She heard some part of Jason creak as he drew closer to her. Blinking rapidly revealed that he was kneeling before her. His large, strong hands came to rest over hers.

"Lianna," he said softly, "what ails you? Are you unwell?"

She shook her head.

"The thread doesn't please you."

" 'Tis lovely," she managed.

"Then what?"

She blinked furiously and wanted to shout at him *What ails me is that being near you gives me a sense of home for the first time in almost a year, and you're too much a fool to notice that you're responsible for it!* She dragged her hand across her eyes to clear them, then glared at him—only to find that he was looking at her with an expression of surprise. And that made her want to slap the look straight from his face.

'Twas no wonder his family skirmished so often.

"Don't you have a crusade to attend to?" she asked shortly.

He studied her closely, wriggling his jaw a time or two as if he considered whether or not he should let it loose and speak.

"Well?" she demanded.

And then he laughed at her.

She growled and gave him a mighty shove. But apparently she was not up to the Artane standards of battle, for she found herself pulled right along with him. Her basket of thread went flying, and she found herself sprawled atop him, having left her dignity and her good sense behind her.

"Let me up, you fool," she said.

"Lianna of Grasleigh," he said, shaking his head in wonder, "you surprise me with your foul tongue. I suppose I should have known your true nature would show itself soon enough."

"If you seek to compliment me," she said, trying to pull away, "you're failing miserably!"

"Then what if I ask you to wed with me?"

It was as if someone had dumped a bucket of winter water on her, so startled was she. She looked down into his face so close to hers and could find nothing to say. He sat up, pushing her back to her knees. He got to his knees as well and took both her hands in his.

"Is the thought so horrifying?" he asked softly.

"Saints, nay," she breathed.

The smile he gave her was so brilliant, she could scarce look at him. She found that she was smiling in return, a smile so wide she felt that her face might split in two. And when he reached up and trailed his fingers over her cheek, she only spared a brief thought for the ruin of her face.

"You are beautiful," he said.

"Nay, no longer."

"Scars mark the passage of battle," he said simply. "I don't see them. I see a woman I love, a woman I want to mother my children, a woman I want by my side for the rest of my days. What are a few scars in comparison?"

"You, my lord, have a remarkable vision."

"And you, my lady—"

"Oh, by all the bloody saints, kiss her, won't you? I can scarce stomach any more of this drivel."

Lianna blinked and looked to her right. Who should be

standing there but Kendrick himself, dressed in normal garb. That was odd enough to merit attention.

"Where are your skirts?" she asked.

Jason laughed heartily, and Kendrick took a step closer, his fists at the ready.

"Nay," Lianna said, holding out her hand, "do not ruin his mouth until he's sealed his offer."

"Did you say him aye?" Kendrick asked.

Lianna looked at Jason. "Mine is not the will you must bend to yours."

"Best kiss her anyway, Jason," Kendrick advised. "It may be all you get."

"Thank you for that," Jason grumbled.

Lianna would have added her thoughts as well, but she found herself suddenly quite occupied, and overcome, by the miraculous event of Jason of Artane taking her face in his hands and kissing her.

And kissing her.

And kissing her yet again.

Indeed, though she was excruciatingly aware of Kendrick standing there making noises of impatience, Jason seemed to take no note of anything but her mouth. And her hair, which he was fingering into complete disarray.

And when he let her breathe again, she wondered if she would ever manage a normal breath again.

"By the saints," Kendrick said in disgust, "that was overdoing it, don't you think?"

"You needn't watch longer," Jason said pointedly.

"Ha," Kendrick replied. "Think you I would leave you alone with her now? The poor girl must have a chaperon, and who better than me to fill those shoes? Take your groping hands off the lass, there's a good lad. Come, my lady, and let me see you safely back to the keep. Your love can press his suit with the king whilst your virtue is still intact."

"Her virtue is safe with me!" Jason bellowed.

"Hrumph. I'll judge that for myself. And how is it you

intend to convince the king to give this prize to a bumbling clod such as yourself?"

"You were supposed to be giving it helpful thought," Jason snapped, helping Lianna to her feet. He gathered up her sewing and his lute, then nodded pointedly at her chair. "Carry that," he said to his brother.

Kendrick looked ready to protest but seemed to think better of it. Lianna soon found herself walking back to the castle flanked by two Artane brothers, who were fighting over her head as to how best win her hand. Jason was holding one of her hands, Kendrick the other. She wondered, as she noted the looks the guardsmen were giving them on their way through the barbican gates, if her reputation would be so ruined that it wouldn't matter who was offering to wed her.

Or perhaps when Maud and her ladies found out whose hands she was holding, she would be too dead for that to matter.

She was left in Kendrick's care while Jason went to stow her stitchery with his gear upstairs. Kendrick found her a place at the table, then sat next to her.

"He agrees with you?" he asked seriously.

The look of earnestness on his face was so surprising she smiled.

"Are you so concerned?"

"Of course. You deserve a happy home, Lianna."

"And you don't think he'll give it to me?"

He did smile then, a rueful smile. "Aye, I suppose he will. 'Tis difficult for me to think of my younger brother being able to do the like, but I suppose he's man enough now."

"But you'll forever look on him as a lowly squire fetching you this and that when you came to visit his master, aye?"

"He told you, then."

"The tortures were described in great detail," she agreed. "And I understand. I could never look at my younger brother that I did not see him as a lad of six or seven, hanging on my mother's skirts."

Kendrick nodded, then looked at her solemnly. "This will be difficult. Whether you'll admit it or not, your lands are vast. The king would prefer to make a more advantageous match for you, no doubt."

"Think you he can be convinced?"

"I've been studying his weaknesses for months. We'll strike at those and see if he cannot be persuaded—"

"By the saints, what filth have we here?"

Lianna blinked in surprise at the harsh voice that cut through their peaceful conversation like a dull knife ripping through linen. She looked at the man who was standing before their table, staring at Kendrick with nothing less than pure hatred.

"Sedgwick," Kendrick said flatly.

"I would call you *Artane,* but that is your brother's right, isn't it?" the other man said. "Have you any title? Ah, how foolish of me to have forgotten. The second son, the one with nothing to call his own but his father's charity."

Kendrick snorted. "William Artane—your memory fails you. My *father,* not my brother, is your father's liege-lord. He will be *your* liege-lord when drink and whoring send your sire to his early death. And then you will be master of Sedgwick, and all the luxury that entails, won't you?"

"At least I'll have a keep," William snarled.

"By my father's charity as well, so that makes you no better than I, does it?" Kendrick returned. "Cousin."

William turned his furious gaze on Lianna. "And who is this? Your latest whore?"

Kendrick rose.

"You're losing your skill, cousin," William said with an unpleasant laugh. "Is this all you could woo to your bed? This pock-marked, uninteresting by-blow of a kitchen lad?"

Lianna watched, open-mouthed, as Kendrick vaulted

over the table and planted his fist in William of Sedgwick's mouth. She watched them push, shove, and hurl insults for several moments before they both drew swords and began hacking at each other.

"By the saints," Jason said, skidding to a halt at her side, "what madness is this?"

"Sedgwick," she said. "He insulted Kendrick."

"What else did he say?" Jason demanded. "Kendrick wouldn't be using his blade for a mere insult to himself." He looked down at her. "Did he say aught to you?"

She winced. "Naught that I haven't heard before."

"Damn," he breathed. "I should have been here."

The herald suddenly bellowed the king's arrival.

"Could matters worsen?" Jason said tightly.

Lianna watched the events before her unfold with a dizzying sense of unreality. Jason sat next to her, clutching her hand under the table, as the king made his way to his place, sat, and demanded a recounting of the dispute.

She listened with growing distress as Kendrick bargained for a chance to see to William on the field. She was certain the king wouldn't allow it. But apparently His Majesty was either overtired or he thought it would make a public example to let the two fight it out, for he agreed.

And then the worst came.

"And to the winner?" the king asked, picking at his tabard. "What prize shall there be?"

"Besides life?" Kendrick asked.

The king looked at him dispassionately. "You fought over a woman. You must value more than just life for that."

"The woman, then," William said. "I'm in need of a wife."

Kendrick opened his mouth to speak, but the king was swifter and his edict was law.

"Lianna of Grasleigh to the one of you who can show

us you're canny enough to win your own life. Then perhaps you'll be worthy of her wealth."

Lianna wished with all her heart that she had a constitution that was prone to fainting, for she would have done it at that moment gladly and not found herself hale and sound and perfectly capable of understanding what had just transpired.

Two men were fighting each other for their lives.

And for her.

While the man she wanted sat next to her, cursing fluently and clutching her hand with enough strength to bruise it.

Eight

Jason stood on the edge of the field next to the woman of his heart and cursed his brother's damned chivalry. And he cursed his own. Had he not been fool enough to trouble himself seeing to Lianna's bloody gear, he would have been in the great hall, ready and willing to avenge his lady for the insults paid to her by that great buffoon, his cousin, William of Sedgwick. Instead, where did he find himself?

Standing on the side of the field, wringing his hands like a woman.

Lianna fared no better, though she seemed to be able to keep herself from wringing her hands. They were clasped together before her so tightly that her knuckles were white. They matched perfectly the pallor of her face.

Jason moved and his mail squeaked. He really should find himself some kind of squire to see to that. Pity he never could find a lord willing to sacrifice his son to Jason's care. Perhaps in time Jason would find himself lord of an obscure keep and some poor lad would come to him then.

Though none of that would matter if he couldn't manage to discover a way to keep Lianna from either Kendrick or William's greedy hands—and he wasn't sure at the moment who would have been worse!

He fingered the hilt of his sword and gave himself over to furious thought. If William prevailed, he could demand a challenge to avenge his then-dead brother, and surely he would emerge the victor. He could worry about his grief over losing Kendrick later. He would have Lianna and repay Sedgwick for Kendrick's death with the same stroke.

Now, if Kendrick won, things would become stickier. How was it one went about challenging one's own brother for the right to a woman? And to the death? His father would surely find that less than pleasing. Then again, he supposed it had been done in the past. Mayhap it could be done in the future.

He heard the clash of metal on metal and realized that Kendrick and William were already at it. Swords, apparently, which gave Kendrick the advantage. Actually, it wouldn't have mattered what the weapon or the battlefield. Jason knew his brother's skill—and he knew what bumbling idiots Sedgwick produced. William would lose, and as his lifeblood drained from him, he would rage about the injustice of having grown up in a keep full of rats, with poor food, and lack of handsome women to bed. That his father was a fool, as his father had been before him, would never enter into the argument. The fault would have lain at Artane that no one there had sent help. Never mind that help would have been summarily rejected.

Jason watched Kendrick fight and found it less exciting than nauseating. His brother was skilled, so skilled that the sight of it should have been enough to give Jason pause. Kendrick had the advantage of five years more training, five years more warring, five years more life on the earth.

But he didn't have the advantage of a desperate desire to wed with Lianna of Grasleigh.

He looked at the field to find Kendrick had gone down on one knee.

But his brother rolled, came up, and cast himself back into the fray without a grunt or a curse. Jason had to admit that it was fascinating to watch the oaf fight, for he did it with the beauty of a dance.

A deadly dance, to be sure.

Time wore on. Jason wished desperately for a very long stick to shove down his back and relieve him of the itch that seemed to have lodged a hand's span below his ribs. The sun beat down on him, leaving him feeling rather like a meat pie, roasting in his mail.

And still the battle continued.

Jason yawned widely, wishing Kendrick would get on with the business at hand. It might have provided Kendrick with amusing entertainment for the morning, but Jason had things to see to.

William, in the end, went down. Kendrick stood over him with his sword at the other man's throat.

"Yield," Kendrick commanded.

"Never," William spat.

"Then die—"

"Nay! I yield, I yield!"

"Coward," muttered Jason. "Like his father before him."

Kendrick pulled his sword away, turned, and went to kneel before the king. Jason closed his eyes and prayed.

Give me a miracle. Just one. I'll never cast another spell.

"Kendrick!"

Jason scarce managed to stop Lianna before she bolted onto the field to save his fool brother, who was near to having himself slain by William of Sedgwick, who had come upon him suddenly from behind. Kendrick rolled, and William's stroke merely grazed him instead of impaling him.

The battle began again, but it was short-lived. With a negligent flick of his wrist, Kendrick sent William's sword flying from his hand. William found himself immediately surrounded and overcome by the king's men who swarmed onto the field.

Jason spared little time wondering what would happen to his cousin. He could have passed the rest of eternity rotting in hell and Jason wouldn't have cared. What concerned him was how he was going to keep his brother from taking Lianna to wife. Could a challenge possibly go wrong?

Kendrick had scarce opened his mouth to flatter Henry before Jason had stepped out into the field, quickly before Lianna could stop him, and strode across to kneel before the king.

"Your Majesty," Jason said, bowing his head, "I challenge Kendrick of Artane for his right to the lady of Grasleigh."

Where there had been low murmuring before, there was a deafening silence now.

Or perhaps that deafness came from the blood thundering in his ears.

Or the waves of Henry's displeasure that washed over him in a thunderous rush.

Jason couldn't tell and didn't dare lift his head to look.

"You, Lord Jason, are not who we would choose for our ward," the king announced in less-than-dulcet tones.

Jason kept his head down. "Artane blood runs through my veins as well, Majesty. I can be an asset and an ally to the crown in the north."

For which his father would blister his ears and likely his arse as well if he could manage it, but there were times a man said what he had to in order to have what he desired. He would be the king's man until it was in his best interest not to be. And with the growing discontent surrounding Henry's extravagant ways, that day could come sooner than Henry might wish.

But for now, he would give as much fealty as his honor would allow and fight his brother for the prize.

Assuming Henry would give him the chance.

It seemed to take the king an inordinate amount of time to come to a decision. Or perhaps he was trying to decide how best to kill Jason so no dark forces were loosed. Jason wasn't sure what the king was thinking, and he didn't dare look up to examine the king's expression.

A sudden and quite ferocious trumpet blast fair gave him a permanently crooked neck from jerking his head up so quickly. Apparently, leave had been granted for him to try to kill his brother.

"To the death, my liege?" Kendrick asked smoothly.

"It seems a pity," the king said thoughtfully, "to lose one of such a fine family."

Jason began to give thanks.

"But all in the name of chivalry, we suppose. Do what you must, my lords."

"Perfect," Jason muttered under his breath as he rose to his feet and looked at his brother.

"I'm bleeding," Kendrick said with what for him was a pout. "Be gentle."

"I'll cut off your head as tenderly as I know how," Jason replied.

"I daresay 'twould grieve our king to lose us both. I'll see that he loses the lesser of us, so his grief is not so heavy."

"I'll play your favorite ballad at your wake," Jason shot back. "And practice much beforehand, that your blighted spirit might not need flinch as you listen."

Kendrick lifted his sword. "A final chance to cry peace and save your wretched life."

"And watch you wed my beloved? I'd rather die."

"Death it is," Kendrick agreed with a regretful sigh. "Yours."

"Nay, yours I'm afraid."

"You could only hope."

"Shall I use the right or the left?" Kendrick asked, studying his hands. "I believe I used to fight you using the left and yet I was still able to best you thoroughly."

"You'll find, my lord, that my skills are much improved. I'd use the right, were I you."

Kendrick smiled, an unpleasant baring of teeth. "No casting of spells, Jas. That wouldn't be sporting."

"I'll brew you a numbing draught to ease the pain as you expire," Jason promised. "Now, be about this business. I've a wedding to see to."

"But no raising of a ghostly ruckus when I take Lianna to wife," Kendrick warned, waving his sword at Jason. "I'll have your word on that now, before I send you to the afterlife."

"You'll be the one doing the haunting," Jason said, flexing the fingers of his free hand and wondering if knifing his brother suddenly would be considered poor manners. At least that way he wouldn't have to listen to any more of Kendrick's incessant chatter.

But then he remembered that such was one of Kendrick's ploys to throw him off guard. And he remembered it the heartbeat before his head almost came away from his neck. He looked at his brother in shock.

"You intend to kill me."

"The king commands it."

"He didn't!"

Kendrick shrugged and continued a very relentless and brutal assault. Jason cast a final look at Lianna before throwing up his sword to avoid another lethal swipe. Kendrick's blade screeched as it traveled the length of Jason's and was stopped by the hilt.

"Fight me or die," Kendrick growled.

"Whoreson," Jason spat.

He wished, absently, that he hadn't said that.

And he wondered, quite seriously, if that might be one of the last things he would regret saying.

Nine

Lianna of Grasleigh, now Lianna de Piaget, still of Gras-leigh, rode next to her newly made husband and wondered just how his parents would take to her, given what it had cost to win her. She fretted, she worried, she twisted her reins in her hands and thought she might be ill. It wasn't just a matter of them acquiring a new daughter-in-law. There was the matter of the life-and-death battle she'd been the prize for not a se'nnight earlier. And the tremendously serious outcome of that battle.

That being the humiliation of one de Piaget brother by another before the king's court, of course.

"Are you well, wife?" came the question from the man beside her.

"Well enough, husband."

"You look nervous."

She looked at her husband of a se'nnight and smiled—nervously. "Will they blame me, do you think?"

"Blame you for what? My victory?"

"Nay, your brother's defeat."

"Does he look defeated?"

She looked to her left to find the aforementioned defeated one, Kendrick of Artane, smiling pleasantly at her. "Don't be fooled," he whispered conspiratorially. "I allowed Jason to win."

"Ha," Jason said scornfully. "Your memory fails you."

"I could not rob you of your love, Lianna," Kendrick continued. "I considered it my chivalric duty to let him win."

Jason snorted. "You've no reason to fear for his ego, my lady. He'll repeat the story for years and end it with you warning him of William's attempted treachery. Somehow he will come away smelling sweetly, and there will be no mention of him kneeling at my feet, weeping for mercy."

"I did not weep."

"Tears were coursing down your face."

"I was sweating."

"You were weeping. And begging. I could not in good conscience slay you."

Kendrick leaned closer to Lianna. "He feared his mother would take a switch to his behind for the deed. I daresay it isn't too late to annul your marriage to him. I am, as you might have noticed, still quite available."

Something whizzed past her nose and connected quite perfectly with Kendrick's. Perhaps there hadn't been much blood on the battlefield before the king, but there was certainly ample draining onto Kendrick's tunic now.

"Damn you," Kendrick snarled, trying to staunch the flow with his sleeve, "can you not fight like a man? Throwing fruit! Who ever heard of such a womanly tactic!"

Lianna found it rather practical at the moment, so she had no argument with it. Kendrick, however, gave his brother a look full of promise and spurred his horse on ahead.

"He's plotting your death," Lianna said wisely, having grown accustomed to the habits of her husband and his brother over the past pair of weeks.

"Aye, likely," Jason said serenely. He looked at her. "Are you happy, my lady?"

"Of course, my lord."

He looked at her for several moments in silence, then his smile faded to be replaced by a look of seriousness.

"Are you?" he asked quietly. "Happy with such a one as I? Henry could have wed you to a man with power and status. I am, as it happens, but the third son."

She shrugged. "What is power but wealth? I daresay you now have enough of that to satisfy any lust you might have for power."

"Aye," he said with a shiver. "Your father had enough of both, and to spare."

"And you wouldn't have known it to look at him. He was much more content discussing pigs than he was bits and baubles for his court clothes. I daresay you'll follow in his footsteps easily enough."

He looked startled enough that she wondered if she'd said aught amiss.

"Jason?"

He shook his head. "Idle thoughts."

"Tell me of them."

"Well, if you must know, the day I arrived at court, I was lamenting the foolishness of courtly conversation that focused on the cut of a tunic or the color of cloth. How much more, I thought, would I have rather been talking to the swineherd about the feeding of his charges, or discussing with the steward whether or not barley and hops might grow well in the north fields, or loitering in the blacksmith's hut to see him at his labors."

"My father would have been pleased with you," she said.

"I could only hope." He reached over for her hand and squeezed it. "If I'm ignorant of something, I'm not too proud to ask for aid. I'll try not to shame you or your sire's memory."

She nodded, but in truth she was thinking less about how he might shame her than she was about how blessed she had been to have found someone with whom she had found a home. For that alone, her father would have loved Jason of Artane. Or Jason of Grasleigh, as it was. The Falcon of Grasleigh, as he would be known. She wondered what he would think when they arrived at her father's keep and she showed him her father's coat of arms.

A falcon with a dragon pinned under its foreclaw. A falcon with its head thrown back in victory.

She could only hope he saw the humor in it she did.

They rode on in companionable silence for the rest of the day. As dusk fell, Lianna was startled to see several men bearing down on them. Jason and Kendrick immediately drew their swords, then Jason called a greeting and was answered in the same tone. Lianna looked at him in surprise.

"Who are they?"

"Our escort," he said. "I'm not surprised to see them, but I am surprised to see them so soon." He leaned on the pommel of his saddle and smiled at her. "What think you of a few days passed in the dragon's lair, my lady?"

Lianna smiled weakly. "These are Blackmour's men?"

"Aye, come to protect his little kit," he said, "and the kit's bride."

"Us?" she asked, feeling rather faint.

"Who else?" He looked at her closely. "Surely you don't fear Blackmour. He is the tamest of men, I assure you. He will merely want to inspect you, see that you have all your teeth, and check that your ears are formed well enough to suit him."

"And should I not suit him?"

"Seven maidens a day before breaking his fast," Jason said with a sigh, "or the occasional consumption of one newly wedded lady. I suppose, then, that if you don't please him, he'll have you for his morning nibble."

She considered her husband. "Your time will come, you know. I daresay you'll be twisting your reins into unrecognizable shapes as we near my home."

"I daresay," he agreed dryly.

"And I will do nothing to ease your suffering."

"Ah-ha," Kendrick called back at them, "you have made your bed, little brother, and see how she smoothes the sheets already. I fear you've met your match in this one."

"And gladly so," Jason said. He smiled at her. "My lord also has a fine chamber for guests with his second most comfortable goose-feather mattress—"

"Not that you've ever slept on it," Kendrick said loudly.

"He," Jason said with a glare at his brother, "will not be accompanying us to your hall, Lianna."

"You'll need someone to guard your back," Kendrick said, "from your lady, should you not show yourself well. 'Tis best I come and see to that. Now, can we be on our way? I've a mind to reach some kind of inn before the sun sets completely."

Lianna looked at Jason. "How much farther?"

"To Blackmour? At least four or five days. These lads have ridden hard to catch us. But I promise you a goodly rest there on that second most comfortable goose-feather mattress I spoke of. And I *have* passed a night or two on it—by myself," he threw at his brother. He smiled at Lianna. "You'll feel comfortable there. You'll see."

It was indeed another five days of travel, but the road was pleasant and the weather fine. Lianna watched Blackmour's men with Jason and saw the respect they accorded him, even though he was much younger than they. She found that by the time they had reached the keep, she had even stopped taking Jason and Kendrick's barbs seriously. There had only been a minor skirmish or two, but Kendrick had very solicitously avoided damaging anything she might find useful.

For herself, she found that being wed to the Dragon's kit was more of a joy to her with each day that passed. He was kind and gentle, and he looked at her with love in his eyes.

What she did find curious, however, was that none of Blackmour's men made any mention of Jason's dark reputation. She had only jested of it once, and by the complete lack of expression on all the faces surrounding her, save Jason who had smiled, she decided that 'twas a subject better left undiscussed.

Except, of course, for the brief moment of privacy she'd had with her husband the morning before they'd arrived at Blackmour when he'd led her off into a small copse of trees for a private kiss or two. When she'd managed to gasp in a breath, she looked at him seriously.

"Have you cast spells?" she asked bluntly.

He blinked, then half of his mouth quirked up in something of an embarrassed smile. "One or two."

"Did they work?"

"We'll have to look at Maud in a year or two and see what's left of her."

She shuddered to think what sorts of torments he had left in place for the women who had dared harm her. Perhaps 'twas best not to know.

"Have you brewed potions?" she asked, determined not to be distracted.

"Aye."

"Studied dark arts?"

He paused. "In a manner of speaking."

"In a manner of speaking?"

He considered for a moment or two. "I have walked blindly into the darkness," he said finally, "and studied art there with my master."

"Have you indeed."

"Aye. Swordplay and such. When you meet him, you'll understand."

"Hrumph," she said, unconvinced. "I vow the only magics you've worked on me are best left for the privacy of our own tent."

"Then you don't think I brewed a potion to make you love me?" he asked, reaching up to tuck a bit of her hair behind her ear. "Or to make you wed with me?"

She pulled him to her and kissed him thoroughly. "Mayhap you brewed aught for me, but my heart was given the moment I saw you, and where my heart was given, my hand was destined to go. Or didn't you know that my father cast his own kind of spell and bound that upon me from an early age?"

"I'll thank him when next we meet, after you and I have spent a very long lifetime together."

"Aye, my beloved nightshade."

He laughed and pulled her close. "Is that how you think of me? What will your people say to that?"

"They'll think me enormously brave to partake of you," she said. "And isn't that your damned brother bellowing for us to return?"

He looked down at her and smiled fondly. "I love you, Lianna."

"And I you, my lord. Now, let us return before I propose a wrestle to silence him myself."

That had been the morning before and she'd found herself too nervous to do aught but give Kendrick a companionable flick on the ear in passing. Now, as she crossed over the enormously small and completely inadequate bridge that separated Blackmour's aerie from the rest of England, she wished she had brawled with her brother-in-law truly. The victory might have occupied her mind enough to cause her to forget her nervousness.

She dismounted in the courtyard. Well, she actually slid from her horse in something of a faint and found herself caught quite deftly by her husband, who set her on her feet as calmly as if he was accustomed to tending swooning wives daily.

They entered the hall, and Lianna soon found herself surrounded by a press of people, adults and children, who couldn't seem to get close enough to Jason. Children tugged at him, cast themselves into his arms, and wept at the sight of him. A handful of lordly men clapped him on the shoulder, and a pair of women greeted him with kisses and affectionate ruffles of his hair.

And then the throng parted.

The Dragon himself—and it could be no other—stood there, waiting with his arms crossed over his chest and a fierce look on his face.

Jason took Lianna's hand and pulled her with him. She didn't want to resist. Not truly. Somehow, though, her heels just seemed to dig into the rushes of their own accord. It was to no avail, of course, for she soon found herself standing far too close to Christopher of Blackmour for her comfort.

"My lord," Jason said, inclining his head.

"So," the Dragon said gruffly, "you found yourself a bride."

"I did, my lord."

"Bested that womanly brother of yours for her, I hear."

"That, too, my lord," Jason said, loudly enough to cover a mighty snort from said womanly brother.

"Let me see her," the Dragon said, "and tell her to stop quivering. I never devour brides until they've slept at least one peaceful night under my roof."

"Oh, Christopher," said one of the women with a sigh.

Lianna looked from the woman, who was shaking her head, then back to the Dragon himself, who seemed to be having trouble maintaining his frown. Perhaps he was tempted to let it disintegrate into something more fierce.

Jason was of no help to her. He stepped aside and placed her hand in the Dragon's talon without so much as a flinch. Lianna swallowed over the hideously dry place in her throat and did her best to stand tall.

"Blonde?" Christopher of Blackmour asked.

Lianna blinked. "I beg your pardon?"

"Dark-haired, my lord," Jason said dryly.

Blackmour grunted. "Her nose is crooked."

Lianna felt her nose with her free hand. It was, as it happened, her best remaining feature. "It most certainly is not," she said, frowning at her host.

"But surely those teeth are rotting."

"My second best feature," Lianna said stiffly, then she realized something that had escaped her attention whilst she was defending what beauty remained her.

Christopher of Blackmour was looking at her.

But he was not seeing her.

She felt her mouth slide open. She gaped at her husband's former master for several moments in silence whilst a pair of things that had never made sense to her suddenly became very clear.

Blackmour rarely left his keep, but the rumor had been because he was too busy practicing his dark arts to do so.

Jason had said his master had taught him to see with his heart, to look beyond what the eye normally was consumed by.

And why not, when his master was blind?

Lianna felt tears well up in her eyes and course down her cheeks before she could stop them.

Christopher of Blackmour sighed. "Now I've made her weep. Gillian, have you a cloth about you for this poor girl? Jason, see what my sweet lady wife has to give you for the tending of your bride. By the saints, this gruff business works so much better when your sire does it."

The woman who Lianna supposed was the lady Gillian snorted in a most unladylike manner. "You've grumbles enough of your own, my lord, and they work well enough. 'Tis but this lady's sweet heart that causes her tears, for I daresay she sees more quickly than most."

She smiled at Lianna, and Lianna found she had an entirely new well of tears to draw upon. What kind of woman was it, she wondered absently, who married a dragon and flourished under his wing?

She suspected 'twas the kind of woman she could only hope to one day become. She accepted Gillian's ministrations, then found herself swept up into a family circle that was so much like her own that it took her breath away.

But it didn't break her heart.

For such a family was now hers.

It was a good deal later that she snuggled with her husband on Blackmour's second finest goose-feather mattress. Having verified its luxury for herself, she could only agree with Jason's assessment of it. She sighed happily.

"This is lovely."

"Aye," he said, stroking her hair with his hand, "it is. I daresay I could not be happier than at this moment."

She lifted her head to look at him. The candlelight flickered softly over his face.

"I never would have guessed his secret," she said.

"He hides it well."

"And you keep it well."

Jason smiled gravely. "He made me the man I am. My gratitude knows no bounds. There is little I would not do for him."

"Or he for you." She made herself comfortable with her head on his shoulder. "I understand he has a present for you. A wedding gift."

"Surely not. What do I need? My own private steward, perhaps," he added with a snort, "to explain to me what I must know to run your father's lands."

"Nay, you'll have me. I served my father often thusly. Your gift is much more precious."

"What is it? And how is it you know of it and not I?"

"You were engaged in spirited discussion of your

brother's faults with your brother and his fists when Lord Christopher told me of it. And to answer your first question, he is sending you something to page."

Jason went very still. "A page?"

"Aye," she said, suspecting very clearly what it would mean to him. "His son, I believe. Surely you know him. Robin of Blackmour?"

Jason was silent for so long, she had to look at him. She leaned up on one elbow and brushed away the tears that had trailed down his temple to wet his hair.

" 'Tis a very great trust," she said quietly.

"From him," Jason said hoarsely, "and your sire as well. I am thoroughly humbled."

She smiled at him, then kissed him briefly. "I'll brew you a potion to bolster your courage."

He grunted at her. "The saints preserve me."

"I met your Berengaria, you know. And her helpers. Nemain and Magda were fighting over who could better teach me what I should know."

"The saints preserve us all," he said fervently.

She laughed and snuggled back down into his arms. "I understand now about your dark arts."

"Do you?"

"Aye. Gillian told me how you and Christopher had trained together, quite often in the dark. With swords, of course."

"Of course."

She paused. "And that is all, isn't it?" she asked suspiciously.

"Of course," he said lightly—and not at all convincingly.

"Jason de Piaget, if you haven't told me—"

But then she found herself pinned by her grinning husband and she was almost distracted enough to forget her suspicions.

Almost.

"I'll count Maud's warts," she warned him.

"You do that," he said with a laugh.

"I'll discover your secrets," she vowed. "All of them."

"May it take a lifetime," he said, bending his head to kiss her. "A very long lifetime with very long days of your constant and thorough scrutiny. Discover away, my love. I could not wish for more."

It was very much later that Lianna had the chance to lie next to her sleeping husband and give thought to the course her life had taken. Who would have known that from such shadows of death, bereavement, and danger at court, she would have come to such a place of light and beauty? She suspected she would be forever inadequate to the task of expressing a proper amount of gratitude for the blessings of family which were now hers. Perhaps a tapestry could be made, one of sunlight and sweet things that grew and flourished. Of course, there would be shadows here and there, for what life was without them?

Especially when one's husband was of the ilk to mutter the odd charm now and again under his breath. And the saints only knew what kinds of things he would put into the cooking pot when not watched closely.

But those were the kind of shadows she could live with, especially when she had Jason of Artane in trade.

She closed her eyes, smiling deeply.

She would begin her stitchery on the morrow.

As soon as it was light.